Holston

William M Kauffman

This book is a work of fiction. It is not the intention of the author to use grammatically correct English language forms in much of the dialogue. Colloquial forms of expression are used extensively. Any resemblance to actual people, places or objects is strictly coincidental.

Copyright
2023 William M Kauffman

For information on the author, see author website:

www.williammkauffman.com

ISBN-979-8-218-33627-1

5.

Ephraim

Ephraim picked up a loaf of Bunny Bread. He squeezed the package; it was soft.

"I think the bakery has just delivered this batch," he thought to himself.

It was Saturday night at Kroger's-about 8:30 p.m. The air outside the store was hot, typical of summer in the American South. The bakery was in the back of the store. Off in the distance, he could hear a rapid popping sound, like firecrackers exploding. Then, there was the sound of glass shattering and a few people shouting hysterically. The lights in the store went out. Everything was silent.

A nauseating uneasiness crept into his mind as he stumbled with his shopping cart through the back of the store toward the checkout stands. It was obvious something serious had taken place. Once at the front, four bodies lay just inside the front door covered in blood. The store manager had been shot in the head and his body lay between the dead shoppers and the cash registers. A young teen-age girl next to Ephraim was making an emotional call to the police on her cell phone. Tragically, it was already too late.

Ephraim felt like throwing up, but he tried to suppress a feeling of panic. He decided to go over and see if he could recognize any of the victims. The stiff body of one of the elders from his church, a frail eighty year old man, lay before him. Ephraim has often seen Glen at the store shopping for himself and his ailing wife, Julie. Tonight, Glen had not been lucky. Ephraim wondered if he should call Glen's wife and tell her that her husband was dead.

6.

"I'll let the cops do that," he decided as he put his cell phone back into his pocket.

"No need to pay for the bread," he thought. "I really need to get back to the house," he reflected.

As Ephraim walked with the loaf of bread to his car, he saw the flashing red lights of two squad cars speeding into the Kroger parking lot. His legs shook slightly as he walked. Once inside his car, he sat for awhile trying to calm down.

"Another killing season in the city had begun," said quietly to himself as he slowly turned the key in the ignition and started the engine.

Once home he noticed that his wife Kim was already asleep in bed.

"No reason to wake her and tell her Glenn is dead," he decided. "Maybe I can find a way to tell her tomorrow morning," he thought.

Ephraim slept fitfully that night. He got up Sunday morning and went into the kitchen. Since his wife was a late sleeper, he fixed his breakfast-Quaker Oatmeal-alone. Their only daughter had moved to Nashville years ago.

"I'll have to call Cindy and give her the bad news about last night at Kroger," he thought.

His daughter, Cindy, had grown up with Glen's daughter, Valerie. The two girls had been in the same Sunday School class for years.

"Glen's family must know all about things by now," he realized.

7.

At 10:45 a.m. as he climbed the steps to the sanctuary, Ephraim grimly reflected that the usual eighty-year-old greeter would not be there to smile and hand him a church bulletin: he had been murdered the night before. The senior pastor, Brian, seemed strangely cheerful he thought, as Ephraim passed him in the vestibule. He entered the sanctuary and sat in his usual pew. To Ephraim, the service that morning seemed surreal, but it passed uneventfully. Brian had chosen the parable of the Good Samaritan for the service. At the end of the service the sanctuary rang to the tune of "Rock of Ages." After the singing of "Rock of Ages" Ephraim felt better.

Tragedy had touched Ephraim's life in the past, but the Kroger shooting was the most direct contact he had with violent crime. Seventeen years earlier, at age fifty-eight, he had been forced out of his job by a supervisor who has falsified his evaluation.

"Bad things happen to good people," his mother had told him once in his teenage years   There was no doubt that his mother had been a very wise woman.

Ephraim was now seventy-five years old. His wife, Kim, was eighty-three. Retirement had been good for him compared to the constant nightmare of his career as a civil servant. Still, he had been proud of his thirty-eight years of public service. By the time Ephraim returned home, Kim had seen the local news and was aware of the demise of their family friend. He greeted her quietly as he entered the living room and sat on the couch in front of the television set. Kim was visibly shaken. "I just cain't bring myself to call Julie," she said in a trembling voice.

"What could I possibly say to her at a time like this?" His wife asked.

"I am gonna call Valerie, Julie's daughter and talk to her," Ephraim said.

After speaking to Valerie, Ephraim felt relaxed for the first time

8.

since the night at Kroger. He decided to take a long nap and try to forget about life.

Ephraim awoke on the couch. It was dark in the living room and the sky was dark outside the living room window. He looked at the clock. The hour hand was at the six o'clock position. Suddenly, he felt disoriented: "was it six in the morning or six at night?" He asked himself. He had no idea how long he had been asleep on the couch nor what day it was.

"Maybe the shootings at Kroger were just a bad dream and the killings never happened," he thought. He stood up from the couch and walked outside. Down the street he saw the lights on at the convenient mart, so he decided to take a walk.

Entering the Road Runner Market his friend, Olga, was on duty. Olga worked the evening shift, so Ephraim realized the time of day was six in the evening.

"The cops picked up Billy and Ed in a big drug bust down by the mall today," Olga mentioned. "The police came by and told me earlier. Those two had forty thousand dollars of cash stashed in the trunk of their car," she said knowingly.

"The cops are good in this town," Ephraim responded. "I had no idea that Billy and Ed were that stupid," he continued. "I hope they like the food at the city jail cause they are gonna be spending a lot of time there," Ephraim responded.

Olga nodded.

"The drink machine is busted again, Ephraim. Ken you believe it?" She asked him.

He looked over at the slim young woman and chuckled a bit. "I saw you workin on it last night. It must have been broken then as well. I stopped by to get a diet coke, but when I saw you foolin with the drink machine again, I left and went down to Hardees," the seventy-

9.
five year old man explained.

"Say, did you hear about the shootings last night at Kroger's?" Olga asked.

The elderly man got the same sick feeling in his stomach from the previous night. "No, I didn't," he said evasively.

Olga had been working the night shift at the convenience store for about three years. She was a single woman, about twenty-six, originally from Moscow. She had been adopted from Russia along with her brother at age eight. The police and a number of single younger men regularly stopped by at night to chat with her during the late hours of her shift. This was probably because she was unusually outgoing and she was also very pretty. She was a slight brunette with wavy hair pulled back and tied behind her head. Like many of the females from Eastern Europe she had an usually clear, pale complexion. Olga took a string mop from behind the counter while Ephraim looked around for something to buy. She wrang the wet mop in a sudsy galvanized bucket and began mopping the floor of the store. Her slight and lithe figure bent over with the effort of cleaning. Ephraim picked up a package of sausage and cheese.

"Olga, I am puttin a ten on the counter to pay for this," he said to her.

She looked up and smiled, "can I keep the change?" She asked.

"You know you ken," the seventy-five year old man exclaimed, and he left the store and walked out into the dark, muggy night.

Several months passed. Summer was nearing its end. Over the intervening months of hot weather there had been several shootings downtown in the early hours of the morning. The police had several suspects, but there had been no arrests. Glen's widow, Julie, had passed away a victim of biliary cirrhosis.

10.
"It's better this way," Kim had admitted to Ephraim the night they were notified of Julie's passing. "Julie hadn't had much of a life for a long time," his wife explained. Valerie, Julie's daughter, had been expecting Julie's end and was therefore emotionally prepared. Somehow, for Valerie, the fact that her father had gone before Julie made things less painful for her.

"Nobody lives forever," Valerie had explained to her own daughter.

Brian, the pastor at Ephraim's' church had been fired for having an affair with a girl who worked in the church kitchen. There had been a nasty lawsuit over the firing, but the church session had held firm on their decision.

Ephraim walked into the kitchen one morning after having driven to Hardees for a diet coke. Kim was up and sitting in her favorite chair in the kitchen. The bright morning light shone through the kitchen windows.

"I brought you this chicken biscuit," he said to her as he handed her the food. "I know you like these chicken biscuits, but you might need to think about eating more vegetables," he said to her.

"Vegetables, that sounds terrible," Kim replied.

Ephraim had always been an advocate of healthy eating, but Kim was a fast food junkie. He knew how addictive the chicken biscuits at Hardees were. He had given in and eaten a butter biscuit himself in the Hardees dining room that morning. Munching on her breakfast, Kim retreated to social media on her cell phone.

Since Kim was preoccupied with social media, Ephraim walked out onto the back deck and sat down in a wicker chair. It was still early morning, so he gazed in the direction of the rising sun off the deck. Light flickered through the boughs of the pine trees separating the sun and the shadows on the floor of the deck. Since he had retired, life had slowed down for him. When his daughter, Cindy, was young and he was working full-time, he and Kim had been living at warp speed.

11.

"I don't know how we managed to keep up with everything," he thought to himself.

Since he had retired, in addition to running around town talking to friends like Olga and a few others, he had taken up music as a hobby.

"The going on the violin is pretty slow," he admitted. The noise he made with the instrument often got onto Kim's nerves and created some trouble between them.

"What does she expect me to do?" He wondered, "spend the rest of my life in a rocking chair?"

To help fill up his time, Ephraim had been attending the men's fellowship at church. Since Brian had been fired, many of the men were not getting along. It was mid-morning in the middle of December and he was sitting at a table in the fellowship hall with three other men and the new pastor.

"I can't stand the color of the new carpets in the sanctuary," Stuart complained. Stuart was a retired Pediatrician.

"The problem with you, Stuart, is that you know everything," Ephraim thought to himself. Ephraim had learned the hard way to keep most of his opinions to himself because of the unpleasantness at the men's fellowships.

"How does everyone like the chicken casserole today?" The new pastor asked.

"It's great. Where did the girls get the recipe?" Ephraim asked.

"Well, it cain't compare to whut my Sally ken make," Fred said. "I think I'll have Sally contact the kitchen staff about the seasonings they are using," he said. The men became quiet as they proceeded

12.

to chew their lunch. After ten minutes of peaceful silence, Tom
picked up his Bible. "Let's have a reading," he suggested.

"Is that the King James version or the Revised Standard version?"
Sam asked. "I ain't listenin to nuthin from sum newish Bible,"
He said firmly. Tom, let's skip the Bible reading and close with a
prayer," the new pastor stated. All the men bowed their heads obediently and waited for the new minister to begin. As the new pastor
led the prayer Ephraim was impressed with him.

"If only these men would listen to this message," he reflected as he
left the fellowship hall.

One Friday night in late December Ephraim drove to Kroger's. It
had been about six months since the shooting. Initially, the shoppers were wary of going to that particular grocery store, but nothing
outlandish had happened since that fatal night. A new manager had taken over. He had been transfered from a large store in
Cincinnati. The new manager had initiated trauma counseling for
the employees. This night Ephraim had been sent for baby carrots,
black bean hummus and pita bread. Not invariably, when he came
back to the store he would have forgotten something. Tonight, he
had put the shopping list on his cell phone to combat forgetfulness.
As he was checking out at the self-service stands, a young woman
began waving at him from the self-service checkout ten feet away.
She looked to be about nineteen and had curly blonde hair.

Uneasy, he looked away, but soon she approached him and looked
straight into his face. "I am the girl you get unsweetened tea from
at Dunkin Doughnuts," she said pleasantly.

He smiled, "oh, I recognize you now. From across the aisle, I
wasn't sure who you were," he said.

"My roommate is Olga from the Road Runner Market," she said.

"Well, tell your roommate to keep all of the old men in line,"

13.

Ephraim said and he smiled.

Ephraim and Olga had talked enough from time to time when he came by the Road Runner for a diet coke that they knew they had much in common. The young woman and the elderly man had siblings who were not good for them.

"Except for my wife and daughter, I can't trust any of my family," he had told Olga one night.

"I haven't spoken to either my mother or my only brother in five years," Olga had related.

"My sister told me one time that she needed money for an operation," he had related. "I gave her six thousand dollars and found out she had breast implants with the money," Ephraim had conveyed.

"I don't know about you, honey, but I am so broke my relatives know better than ask me for money. Frankly, when they call, I have to hang up on them," she had said.

It was early one Wednesday morning in January. Ephraim had awakened at six. He could never lay in bed for hours like Kim and Cindy. He made his oatmeal and took the car down to Hardees to get an iced tea through the drive-in window.

"This one is on me, baby," the young female clerk said as she handed him a cup of iced tea through the drive-in window.

Since Ephraim was a frequent customer of Hardees, sometimes three or four times a day, he often got food and drinks for free. Back at the house, he walked into the darkened downstairs bedroom and turned on the lights. This room was his music room.

He had been exiled there after months of practicing his clumsy music upstairs while Kim and Cindy watched television. After thirty minutes struggling with some new sheet music, he heard Kim's

14.

foot pounding on the floor of their bedroom above.

"Time to put up the fiddle and listen to music through my head-phones," he acknowledged to himself.

By noon his interest in music had ebbed. He took down a volume of John Steinbeck's "East of Eden" and began to read. The story of Adam who had unwittingly married a prostitute was interesting. Ephraim found it hard to believe that this man's wife would shoot the husband who took her in and cared for her, only to reenter the world's oldest profession in a neighboring town.

"Go figure," he thought to himself. "I have never understood wom-en-folk," he said. He looked at the picture of John Steinbeck on the back of the novel.

"He was one ugly man," he thought to himself. "Don't matter how famous he was," Ephraim reflected, ,"only a woman with his sorry looks would give him a second glance," he reflected. "I ain't no prize winner mysell," he thought. "But I am a good sight more at-tractive than that guy," Ephraim promised himself.

At age seventy-five, with his flagging energy level, aches and pains, he wondered why the young girls liked talking to him.

"Am I really that great, or do these young gals just feel sorry for me?" He asked himself. "Don't matter anyway; any one of them who wants me as a friend will get her wish. I am pretty sure, though, not one of them think I look that good," he said to himself. "When yer over the hill," he thought, "you take kindness no matter where it comes from."

The rest of the afternoon was spent meditating on these many issues of his retired life. By early evening, Kim had finally gotten up and was sitting in the kitchen drinking coffee.

"Think I'll mosey on down to the Road Runner," he told Kim as he put on his jacket and headed toward the garage door.

15.

Olga rang up an order from a middle-aged man dressed in rags. "He looks like he might be homeless. How can someone get into that kinda shape?" She wondered to herself.

Her friend, Ephraim, had just stopped by for a fountain drink and then chatted for a few minutes. To Olga, being adopted and then estranged from her adoptive parents, Ephraim was the caring male figure that had always been missing from her life. Younger boy-friends, like the adoptive parents, had not been supportive either.

"Except for Ephraim, they all have something they want from me," she bitterly reflected. "Takers, not givers," she thought.

The young brunette's thoughts were interrupted by the distinct groaning of the deforming of metal. There was a sudden noise along with the groaning, but before she noticed the sound, it had ceased. She peered out of the front window of the Road Runner Market to see a Ford RAM 500 truck on top of a small gray sedan. She took out her cell phone, dialed 911, and reported the accident to the police dispatcher.

Within five minutes, the first police cruiser had arrived to investigate the accident. Soon a noisy ambulance had arrived. The flashing lights of the emergency vehicle lit up the night as Olga walked out-side to investigate. The RAM truck was pulled off the sedan. The sedan was totaled with the driver trapped inside. The young wom-an noticed that the interior of the windshield of the crumpled sedan was covered in red blood.

"How is he, the poor man?" Olga asked the officer directing things.

The officer looked up and quietly shook his head. The driver side door was soon pried open and the EMT's carried the unfortunate motorist off strapped into a rolling stretcher.

"Do you know this guy?" The officer asked Olga as he took the vic-tim's driver's license out of a wallet and handed it to her.

She felt confused and her vision blurred. In order not to collapse, she slowly lowered her body to the ground and placed her hands on the parking lot surface to steady herself on all fours as the attack of vertigo progressed. After ten minutes, the attack was over and Olga stood up. The police and ambulance were gone. The night was quiet and still. Only the RAM truck remained with its steering wheel locked. A young male driver sat inside the truck awaiting a tow. Olga walked over to the driver inside the cab on unsteady legs. She noticed that he didn't seem a bit ruffled by the scene that had occurred.

As she looked into the driver's face, he quietly spoke: "I didn't see him."

Anger welled up into the mind of the woman. She stuttered loudly, "you didn't see him....you didn't even look!" She nearly shouted.

She found herself clutching the side of the truck door ad scratching at the paint erratically.

"You are a maniac driver...You drive like a crazy man!" She said in a hoarse voice.

Ephraim lay paralyzed with drugs on a respirator in the local intensive care unit for six days. No visitors were allowed. He had sustained closed chest trauma and multiple internal organ lacerations during the wreck at the Road Runner Market. Prior to being transferred to the intensive care unit he had been in surgery for eight hours. The doctors told Kim and Cindy that at age seventy-five, they were unsure he could survive the severe injuries. Slowly, his vital signs stabilized and his blood pressure came under control without medication. After one week he was weaned off the respirator and transferred to the step-down unit.

Twelve months passed. Olga, as usual, worked Friday night at the Road Runner Market. Since the night of the car crash with the RAM truck, she had not seen her friend Ephraim. She was painfully aware why he was no longer around. She had recognized his picture on the driver's license of the critically ill motorist. She had given up Ephraim for dead.

"If he were alive, he woulda come by to talk by now," she had told herself.

Her life had become dreary, and each passing day was another burden for her to bear. On this particular night, she had her back to the store front as she was stocking cigarettes behind the counter.

As she worked with her back to the store front, there was a loud rustling sound in the far corner of the store. Someone was inspecting packages of potato chips. She heard the customer cough as he walked up to pay for the package of chips. Turning around, she saw him pushing a steel walker steadying himself to pay for the chips. He was very thin, and his eyes bulged slightly with the look of chronic illness. The man's face broke into a wide smile.

"Baby, is that you, Ephraim?" She stuttered.

All the sorrow of the past year surfaced and she began to weep.

Then, looking up at her frail friend through blurred vision, she said, "honey, you are a miracle."

18.

19.

Dana

Freddy worked after school in his dad's farm supply store. He was
a junior at Mayfield High School. It was a good job and it was en-
joyable. Many of the local farmers and their families were customers. His father's store was a family enterprise and Freddy quickly
became friends with the regulars. One of his favorite jobs at the
store was loading feed into the trucks for their rural clientele. This
was how he met Dana. She was a sophomore at the same high
school that Freddy attended. Her father had been a carpenter and
a part-time hog farmer. Mr. Gorely had bee absent from home for
several years. Dana, her sister Libby and their mother Fran were
keeping things together without him.

The Gorely women were definitely all related: blondes of medium
height with strong, well-molded figures. Dana was the shortest of
the three, about five-foot three inches. She had a friendly smile,
brown eyes, and a lightly freckled face. Dana handled all the money and was the Gorely woman who purchased the hog feed. The
Gorely women were conservative and always paid in cash. One
Friday evening, as the farm store was closing, Dana approached
the cash register.

"One hundred pounds of swine pellets," she chirped.

Freddy rang up the swine pellets and reached out for the money.
As the twenty dollar bill approached Freddy's hand, Dana's fore-
finger gently swept across his hand. She then looked up into his
eyes, turned away and walked back through the store toward the
steps outside the back of the store down to the loading area of the
basement. Freddy's look followed her figure. He felt a twinge of
admiration as he noticed the curves of her body surrounded by the
evening sun.

On Saturday, the store closed promptly at six o'clock. It was seven-thirty one evening and Freddy was upstairs in his parent's house
when his mother called up to him. There was a girl on the phone

20..

asking for him.

"This has never happened before," he thought as he picked up the telephone receiver.

It was Dana. Next Saturday was visitor's Sunday at the Highland Chapel and she would be pleased if Freddy would accompany her and her sister Libby to church.

"Uh, sure," he replied. Freddy began to search for something further to say, and after a short pause, Dana's voice returned to the phone.

"Great, Freddy, then we will pick you up at ten a.m. Sunday week at your house," she said.

Freddy returned the telephone receiver to its holder and grimaced about how ungainly he thought he appeared to girls. He thought that he was definitely too tall and thin, and he had ugly, red hair.

Sunday week the Gorely women picked Freddy up in their blue Ford sedan promptly at ten a.m. Fran and Libby were in the front seat and Dana sat in the back with Freddy. The trip to Highland Chapel was a relatively short drive into the countryside. The church building was over one hundred years old, having been built just after the Civil War. It was an attractive white frame building, but it did not have air-conditioning. The pews were old, but in good shape and a varnished wood railing separated the congregation in the pews from the pulpit. Fran, Libby, Dana and Freddy sat on two rows to the left of the center aisle.

As the Gorely women and their guest sat, the guest was noticing his date. Dana sat stiffly at his side. Her blonde hair was pulled back into a ponytail, revealing the curve of her forehead. She wore a knee-length, floral print dress and white, patent leather shoes.

21.

As the service wore on, Freddy's mind was predominantly on Dana. He had decided that her pink lips and white legs were her most out-standing features. In the midst of this reverie, he began to hear a banging noise from the pulpit. Allie D., the minister, was pounding the podium with his fists.

"He lives!" Allie D. shouted.

"Amen," a portly woman from a back pew answered while cooling her face with a hand held cardboard fan.

The minister preached that, despite the passage of over two thou-sand years since the crucifixion, Jesus was still coming back to save believers.

Freddy looked over at Dana's angelic face, "yes," he affirmed, "Je-sus will definitely come back in his own time.

As church was letting out, Dana thanked Freddy for being her guest with a smile and gentle pressure on his arm.

Weeks later, Freddy was passing a huddle of teen-age girls at the high school, when he noticed two of the girls look his way. He craned his neck to see who was in the middle of the huddle, when a shapely hand waved over at him. He looked further; yes, it was Dana. Returning to the lunch room alone, he racked his brain over where he could take Dana out for a date. He knew that if he didn't do something soon, she would probably not make another move on her own,

"Every girl has her pride," he thought.

Finally, he decided to ask Dana to a softball game at the city park the following Tuesday night. After a nervous two days, he managed to make the call and he was relieved when she said, "yes."

22.

Tuesday night Freddy parked his pickup at the ball park with Dana sitting in the front seat near him. One of Dana's friends ran over and peered through the open truck window.

"C'mon....The game's just starting," the friend said.

Night softball games were the most exciting event in town. By the time the game began, the heat of the day had subsided and the floodlights gave the ball field a party like atmosphere. On this night, the Murray Jets were going up against the Mayfield Mavericks. After six innings, the Jets were ahead by four. After seven innings, the score was nine to three.

Sometime after the game had started, Dana left the bleachers to join the crowd below the stands. Voices became animated as the kids shared stories from school. Later, a few older boys joined the group. Freddy began to miss his date. He caught sight of her just as one of the older boys, Bret, joined in conversation with Dana. Freddy knew this guy. Bret was two years Freddy's senior and he was a freshman at the community college. Bret had begun hanging around the high school girls.

"He has that smug, college boy look," Freddy muttered as he made his way over to Dana.

By the time he arrived, Bret was right up next to Dana. Upon seeing Freddy, she nudged him playfully with her hips and encircled one of his arms in hers. They then left to sit together through the remainder of the ball game. The Jets won.

For the rest of the year, Freddy and Dana were an item. He had lettered in cross country and she proudly wore his jacket. Through-out the winter weekends, they were regulars at all of the basket ball games, and they often went to the Dairyette together for hamburg-ers after the games.

The school year drew to a close and summer began. In order to

23.

keep up with each other, Dana had invited Freddy to the Gorely
farm in June to pick black berries. The weather was hot the Monday Freddy drove up her driveway in his pickup. Dana met him at
the porch with two, one gallon plastic pails. The Gorely farm consisted of forty acres: twenty acres of grassland and twenty acres
of woods. Behind the house was a barn and a pig lot. Behind the
barn was a small pond. Nearby was the black berry patch. The
berry patch had existed for years and consisted of older, stunted
plants with thick stems and tall young plants that sprouted the larg-
est berries.

Dana showed Freddy how to bend back the stems of the black
berry bushes and carefully pick the fruit without getting scratched.
After their pails were full, they lay down beneath a grove of young
trees to cool off. The sage grass under the trees cushioned the
young people as they lay near each other. Soon it was time to
head back to the house. Fran was expecting the pair to join her
and Libby for a snack.

Fran took the pails from Dana and Freddy and dumped the berries
into a large enamel sink. The berries were rinsed and placed in
four bowls sitting on a checkered tablecloth. The four sat eating.
Fran, Libby and Dana talked over farm issues. Freddy was quiet.

"How are your hands?" Fran asked Freddy. He looked down at the
numerous scratches and bug bites on his skin.

At the end of the visit, Dana walked Freddy to his pickup truck. She
raised her face for a parting kiss, and then happily walked back to
the farmhouse.

After that June day, Freddy stopped calling Dana. June became
July and then August arrived. Still, he did not call her. "I am much
too busy," he told himself. "School and work are taking all my time,"
he thought.

24.

When Freddy was not working at the store or attending class, he was at cross country practice. Dana had become conflicted and worried, but she would not call him. She started sending Libby up the back stairs of the farm supply store to pay for the animal feed when they came to the store. Finally, one Saturday Dana got into the blue Ford and drove to the farm supply alone.

Slowly and with effort, the young girl climbed the steep stairs up the back of the store. As she walked through the store, she caught sight of Freddy standing behind the cash register. When he saw Dana approaching, Freddy turned his head to stare out the front window. Freddy looked everywhere except at Dana.

Tears filled Dana's eyes and she started to call out to him... "Freddy," but she stopped herself. She slung his cross country jacket onto the counter in front of him, turned and walked away.

1

25..

26.

Trudy and Arthur-In Three Parts

27.

Part One

It had been a very long day at the smoothie shop. Trudy's boss,
Amy, had been in a bad mood and had left hours before. "Soon, it
will be ten o'clock and time to close up," Trudy thought. Trudy was
twenty-eight and single. She was medium height, about five-foot
five inches. Her supple frame was on the slight side, but her girlfriends told her that she was beautiful

"All this beauty stuff," she thought. "They are just trying to be kind,"
she told herself. It was Friday night as she counted the bills and
coins in the cash register.

A solitary man sat in the corner of the shop finishing his drink. He
tried not to stare at Trudy, but she had a quality that interested him.
He turned around and took a long look at her. Her medium length
blonde hair curved under a feminine jaw, just below her rounded
cheeks. Her hair was light; her eyebrows were dark.

"She is striking to look at," the man thought. "I would bet five dollars she is smart and can hold her own with any single man," he
thought, sitting silently.

Outside the strip mall that housed the smoothie shop it was a dark
summer night. Arthur was the last customer of the day. He was de-
laying leaving the shop so he could keep sneaking peaks at Trudy.
This was no secret to the twenty-something woman as she shut the
register drawer and walked to the front of the shop placing her hand
on the light switch. She quickly switched the overhead lights on
and off rapidly to notify the man that it was time to go.

As Arthur rose from his seat from a back table and ambled toward
the front, Trudy noticed that he was not particularly well-dressed.
He had on plain, brown slacks with stove pipe trouser legs and a
green, short-sleeved cotton shirt. She opened the door as he

28.

exited, noticing coffee stains on the front of his shirt.

"Come back, sir," she said quietly.

Arthur looked back over his shoulder as he stepped onto the concrete sidewalk. "Are you working tomorrow?" he asked as he
looked into her green eyes. Trudy quickly shut and locked the door
without answering. She retreated through the darkened shop to the
rear service exit.

Arthur ambled slowly through the parking lot to his old car. Pulling
his car onto North Roan Street, he turned left and headed toward
the south side of town. The city had done a good job of keeping the
streetlights working. Even the shabby parts of town were well-light-
ed. As he approached the city library going south, there was a
young woman standing on the sidewalk near the building, alone.
Since it was a summer night, she was dressed in a short, bright
blue single piece dress with an upscale sliver bag hanging from one
shoulder.

"Not bad looking," Arthur reflected as his car passed slowly by her.

The woman waved to the single man in the car. The single man's
gaze reverted from the woman to the front of the car. He did not
stop, but continued toward the old brick buildings of downtown.
Crossing Main Street, he noticed that the new condominiums were
still up for sale. Sadly, graffiti defaced the front of the condominium
complex with broad strokes of red paint.

Trudy locked the rear service exit of the shop and walked through
the back lot. She felt inside her purse to make sure her mace was
inside.

"You can never be too careful," she thought as she gripped the
strap to her purse. Each night, whenever it was time to leave, she

29.

felt unease creep down her back as she walked to her car. Nervously, she stepped inside her car and pushed the door lock down. Only then, when she was inside the car with its door locked, did she feel relieved.

At this time, Arthur was forty-one years old. He had never been married. It was not that he didn't like women, but he never had what he thought would make him an acceptable husband. He had spent his single life perpetually broke.

"I cannot support a wife when I can barely feed myself," he had acknowledged. "Another thing," he had realized..."Pursuing women of loose morals could lead to entrapment into an unwanted marriage should one of them accidentally become pregnant. "I better stay celibate," he reflected.

He had made good on this promise to himself, yet because of it he lived a life of misery. Arthur was poor, but ethical and moral. Even so, he avoided attending church because he was constantly haunted by "unholy" thoughts about women.

Arthur parked his car behind a second-hand trailer that he owned and lived in. Carefully, he locked the door to his Ford and walked up the unpainted wooden steps and stood in front of the aluminum door. He turned the key in the lock, opened the door and walked inside. The air inside was uncomfortably hot.

"I don't hear the window unit blowing," he realized.

Once in the back room, where he slept, his worst nightmare came true. The room air-conditioner was broken. He retreated to the kitchenette and pulled a TV dinner from the refrigerator and heated it in a plastic microwave oven. The food in the TV dinner tasted like cardboard to the forty-something man.

30.

"No reason to complain," he reflected.

Going out to eat was a rare treat for Arthur. He spent most of his dining-out hours in the smoothie shop sipping the cheap, fruity drinks.

"A full meal out could cost over thirty dollars," he had learned.

Two weeks later, Trudy sat in the Market Street Diner with her friend Elena. Elena worked at Sanchez Grocery. It was ten o'clock on a Monday night and both women sat before grilled chicken sandwiches with fries and a drink.

"The men in here are creepy," Elena said looking up from her breaded chicken sandwich. "Look down and don't let them see you staring, otherwise one might come over and try to chat us up," Elena advised Trudy.

At the corner table across the diner, a tall thin man with a ghostly white complexion and long, stringy black hair snuck glances at the two women.

"That one looks pretty hard up for a girl if you ask me," Elena whispered.

"He's the type you might see parking his car at the strip club on the south side," Trudy said.

"That's disgusting," Elena answered.

"Look honey...We all got the same urges; it's just that some of us do something about it. He might be a guy that likes to look, but won't touch," Trudy said.

"Looking...That's the first step," Elena warned. "Next thing you know

31.
he'll try to put his arms around something that won't say no," she said.

The evening after Trudy and Elena ate sandwiches at the diner, Trudy stopped by the Pit Bull Gym on Main Street in Greenville. She had been a member for five years and she had tried to get Elena and Beth to join. Elena and Beth had made excuses not to join: exercise did not fit into their schedules. Beth was an over-worked nurse at the medical center, and Elena just could not get up the energy to go out once she was home from her job at Sanchez Grocery. It was nine-thirty p.m. and the slim, bleached blonde was lifting weights along one of the brick walls of the gym.

A pudgy, middle-aged man stood across the gym from her on a stair-master. Trudy could sense the sweat pouring out of the soft face of the out-of-shape man. He had been noticing Trudy for some time. There were many shapely, single women at the gym, but Trudy worked out more regularly than most of the others. The older man looked admiringly at the curves of her hips and legs as she stood pulling down weights suspended from a roller and cable.

"All the women her age look good," the man thought. "There was a time when I could have had a date with something like that, but that was years ago," he told himself. "The hot young girls are for the hot young guys," he reflected.

After she had finished exercising for the night, Trudy made her way to the rear corner of the gym to avoid the gaze of her admirer. She bought a bottle of cold water from a machine, and put her towel into a plastic shopping bag. Then she made a quick exit. Driving back to her apartment, the twenty-eight year old's mind began to wander.

"Why am I so unhappy?" She thought. "I have a good job at the smoothie shop; I have my own car, and I have friends like Elena and Beth who can be trusted," she thought.

32.

She thought about Arthur, who had tried to talk to her a few weeks before as she closed up one night. Once in her apartment, she sat down in her easy chair and picked up a magazine. She gazed through the pages of perfect men and women living a perfect life. In time, she threw the magazine on the floor beside the chair and went to bed.

Since the night Arthur had seen Trudy, he had become beset by problems. He had discovered after arriving home from the smooth-ie shop that the window air-conditioner had broken down. The next day, a lanky, older repairman met him at the trailer. The repairman typified service workers in the Greenville area. He lived in a neigh-boring town where the cost of living was much lower. People in those towns resented the ones living in the larger towns where Ar-thur and Trudy resided. Not only did they resent the more monied classes, but they disliked aimless younger people. Bob mumbled to himself as the took the compressor motor apart and inspected it.

"Why ain't you married mister?" He said abruptly. "You one a these kinda guys that like boys instead of these pretty girls?" Bob asked rudely.

"Just do your work. I don't answer questions like that," Arthur snapped.

"Yer kind are goin to Hell fer yer evil deeds," Bob said.

"You are done here, buddy. Tell me now, what is wrong with this thing?" Arthur said.

"That'll be one hundred dollars or you ain't gettin rida me," Bob replied.

Arthur grimaced as he handed over the bills. Bob walked over to his truck and put his tools into a large tool box in the front of the bed of the pickup.

33.

You can go to Walmart and get something that is gonna work," he said as he climbed inside the cab and turned the motor on.

Arthur watched the smoke from the exhaust pipe of the sturdy truck as it exited the driveway of the trailer park.

Two weeks later Arthur was finishing the workday at Zack's Chicken. He had been the second shift supervisor for seventeen years.

"I don't really like chicken, but if they are giving me free food here, I am going to eat it," he told himself after his shift as he ate a two-piece white meat dinner.

Later, he left for the day. The air was hot and dry that night. There had not been much rain for weeks. Driving with the windows of his car open, the air from the city blew into his face. He pulled the car beside the smoothie shop.

"I could use a little cooling off before I go back to the trailer," he thought as he climbed out of the car and shut the driver-side door.

He reached into the back pocket of his pants and drew out a plastic comb he had bought at CVS drug store. He combed his hair into a semblance of order and walked inside the smoothie shop.

Arthur approached Trudy as she stood, hunched over while filling a large bin with ice cubes from the commercial refrigerator in the back.

"Mango-Magic," he said looking straight into the bleach-blonde woman's face. He noticed the black roots of her hair. "Where do you get your hair done? Looks nice," he said.

"Can I get you anything else, beside the Mango-Magic?" Trudy said without answering his question.

"No," he said and he then sat down at a table to wait for the smoothie.

When the smoothie arrived, Arthur looked up and asked, "ever eaten at Zack's Chicken on North Roan? I am the second shift supervisor there," he said with emphasis.

"Well, the chicken is pretty good at Zack's. You have my compliments," she told him.

"If you will meet me there for lunch tomorrow, I will treat you," he offered.

"I guess that would be okay. How bout I get there about twelve noon," she said trying to affect a lack of real interest.

'You won't be sorry," Arthur said as he stood to leave. "We got a new shipment of fresh chicken just today," he concluded as he opened the glass door and walked outside.

The day of the date between Arthur and Trudy, Arthur had risen from bed early. His usual shift at Zack's began at three p.m. and lasted until eleven p.m. As a result, he would be free when Trudy met him at noon for lunch. He woke at eight o'clock that morning, and once getting out of bed, he began searching for clothes to wear.

"My usual work pants will not do," he reflected.

Sixty minutes later he was standing before a clothes rack in the Greenville mall inspecting a new pair of pants. Arthur was on the thin side, and in his opinion, most pants hung awkwardly from his hips.

35.

"I can't change the way I look, so maybe new pants will help," he thought as he grabbed a pair of tan dress pants and walked back to the dressing room.

His closet at the trailer was filled with pants he had bought at Plato's-the used clothing store across North Roan from the smoothie shop. He had always bought new, attractive shirts for work, though.

"I better get a decent, black leather belt," he said to himself as he chose one and proceeded to the counter for pay for the pants and belt.

Noon found Arthur sitting at a small table in Zack's. He looked up as Trudy walked in through the front door.

"She is too good-looking for me," he thought glumly.

He noticed the shapeliness of her athletic legs below a short, green skirt with black polka dots. To compliment the skirt she was wearing a white blouse with a frill front. The skirt showed off her narrow waist. Arthur stood up and smiled, looking directly at his date. Quickly, he walked around the table and helped her into her chair.

Trudy held out her hand, which Arthur took in his and said, "I am Trudy McIntosh."

He replied, "I am Arthur Reagan."

The not-so-young singles ordered their meals and began to chat while they ate. Trudy inspected Arthur with her discriminating green eyes. He was thin and an average-looking forty-something man. He had short brown hair combed to the side and blue eyes.

"Fortunately, Arthur's nose is not that big," she reflected.

"His front teeth are a little crooked, but not that bad," she thought. "He has nice clothes," she acknowledged.

By the end of the meal, Arthur had passed muster in Trudy's eyes and she had decided, at the very least, they could be friends. Taking the lead as Arthur paid the bill, she gave him her number and he quickly scribbled his number down and gave it to her.

"Are you coming by the smoothie shop this weekend?" Trudy asked him.

"Of course I am. I'll be there Saturday night," he responded.

Trudy and Elena sat sat the Market Street Diner the next week for a Wednesday lunch.

"Tell me about your new man," Elena said as the two women sat before vegetable soup and sweet tea.

"He's not my man, Elena: we're just friends," Trudy answered.

"Maybe you see things that way, Trudy, but he has got to have other plans," Elena said.

"He works at Zack's as the second shift supervisor," Trudy explained.

"I know that guy...I have been at Zack's allot lately. He's the skinny guy with short hair, isn't he?" Elena asked.

"That's him. He stops by the smoothie shop on Saturday nights," Trudy revealed after swallowing a spoonful of soup.

"You aren't wearing any really short skirts to work, are you?" The grocery store clerk demanded. "Look, Trudy, you better be careful," Elena pleaded.

"I don't think he will be a problem...So far there have been no warning signs with him," the woman with the black eyebrows explained.

Since the meeting of Trudy and Arthur at Zack's Chicken, the second shift supervisor had been stopping by the smoothie shop each Saturday night about ten o'clock. A certain attractive blonde woman was always working at that time. As a loner, Arthur had not had much experience with women, despite the fact that he was pushing forty. One night, as he sat sipping his usual mango smoothie, his friend suddenly sat down at his table and faced him. Arthur was accustomed to the verbal banter from the counter as Trudy worked. This was new territory.

"How...How has your day gone, Trudy?" He stammered.

She smiled to herself, "he needs some help," she thought.

If there was one thing Trudy was good at, it was talking. She happily reviewed her good and bad clients for the day and the ups and downs of working for Amy. Arthur sat watching her face engaged in conversation. His attention became fixed on her lips as they moved with each word.

"Her lips look really soft," he thought. "What would it be like to touch them with my lips?" He asked himself. Trudy had a curvy smile and thick lips accentuated by the latest fashion in lipstick. "If I keep staring at her face, she is going to think I am strange," he thought. He then began staring off into the corner of the room.

Trudy noticed immediately as her male friend looked off into the corner of the room.

38.

"Am I really that boring?" She asked herself. Testily, she spoke, "are you tired Arthur? Have you had a long day?"

The man who had been lost in thought about this woman, did not appear to hear what Trudy said. She reached her tapered index finger out and poked him in the arm. As he turned back and looked at Trudy, he was confronted with his feelings for her: feelings that had been growing stronger over the past few weeks.

"Sorry, Trudy," he said with distraction in his eyes.

"You finish this smoothie, honey, and then you can walk me to my car," she said.

Arthur came to himself and began swallowing the remaining contents of the paper cup. He stood up awkwardly and let her lead him out of the shop into the back parking lot. Stopping at her car, Trudy put out her hand for a handshake. Arthur hastily took her hand in his. Trudy smiled and opened her car's door and climbed inside.

39.

Part Two

Arthur sat alone in the trailer. It was midnight, one hour after his
shift at Zack's Chicken had ended. His mind was filled with the
chaos of the day. One of the new cooks in the kitchen had called in
sick that day.

"As second shift supervisor, I do all the things no one else will do,"
he had complained as he had donned and apron and busily began
putting a basket of frozen fries into a vat of hot grease. The grease
sputtered and small drops of it flew into the air and landed on his
clean blue shirt. Within an hour the shirt was filthy. His short brown
hair stood on end and sweat dripped from his face onto the counter.
He hurriedly breaded a batch of chicken pieces.

That night in the trailer the forty-one year old shook his head to
clear away thoughts of the chicken restaurant. Across the room
of the trailer Arthur imagined that he could see Trudy sitting in the
dark. He looked intently at her.

"What are your thoughts, Arthur?" She asked. Arthur shuddered.
His thoughts were not honorable.

He turned his head to avoid her stare as the image of her torso,
sitting erect, consumed him. For months now, he had wanted to
take her in his arms and press her close to him. He turned his head
back to face her. He then could see himself standing beside her,
brushing his fingers against her cheek and pulling her blonde hair
back behind her ears.

Greenville was a troubled city. Each summer the shootings downtown left victims: both alive and dead. Most of the incidents were
drunken fights gone awry. The shooters were always men and the
dead were men. Living victims were both male and female.

40.

"This does not say much for humankind," Arthur thought sadly one day. "Really, too many men are violent," he reflected.

Most of Arthur's friends owned guns. It was Wednesday night and he sat at the Apex Bar with an unsweetened tea before him on the counter. To his left was an over-weight man in a tee-shirt and with a baseball cap turned backward on his large head.

"Why don't you drink a man's drink?" The man said loudly into Arthur's ear.

The man put his large arm out in front of the chicken cook, picked up the unsweetened tea, and poured it out onto the wood of the bar. Arthur had never been in a fight.

"Am I a coward or do I just know when to quit?" He asked himself as he scooted his stool back, stood up and walked toward the exit.

"Yer a sorry ass excuse fer a man!" The big man shouted at him as he passed through the door.

As Arthur drove to the trailer after leaving the Apex Bar, he could hear police sirens in the distance. Quickly, he found himself being followed by a squad car. Soon he was pulled over. Arthur sensed a feeling of dislike growing in him as the officer approached his driver's side window.

"May I see your license and car registration?" The burly officer asked abruptly.

After the officer had inspected both documents, he advised Arthur to drive carefully, get off the road and go home. Back in his trail-er, Arthur wondered why he had heard so many police sirens that night. Switching on his small radio, he found his answer: a twenty-six year old man had been gunned down that night outside the

41.

Road Runner Market on West Market Street. He then turned off the radio and overhead light and climbed into bed.

That night Arthur could not sleep. He had bought a new air conditioner from Walmart. The new machine made a loud humming noise that could be heard throughout the trailer. The window near his bed was just beneath a streetlamp outside on a tall pine utility pole. The stark light of its lamp shone into his face. In order to fall asleep, he closed his eyes tightly and turned over in his bed facing the side opposite the window. The cold air in the trailer was damp. The new air conditioner was doing a poor job removing water vapor from the humid air of the east Tennessee summer. Sometime after three o'clock in the morning, he finally dozed off.

Two weeks later Trudy and Arthur were sitting at the Market Street Diner. Trudy was contemplative that night. Elena had known the man who had been murdered earlier at the Road Runner Market and she had shared this with Trudy. News of the killing was widespread throughout Greenville. Trudy had ordered Mexican chili and Arthur was munching on a chicken quesadilla.

"Trudy isn't saying much," Arthur worried. He reached over and began sprinkling crumbles of saltine crackers into her chili. "My mom always put crackers on top of chili," he offered. "Try it," he suggested.

Trudy looked up, "the dead man at the Road Runner Market was Elena's friend, Arthur," she said. "His wife beat up another woman with a taser thinking the woman had put some man up to the killing of her husband," she said looking into her date's eyes. "There is some woman behind all the bad things men do," Trudy concluded. She looked down and stirred her chili.

"You are behind every good thing that I do, Trudy," Arthur said earnestly taking her hand in his. Trudy quickly withdrew her hand in confusion. "Is something wrong?" He asked her.

42.

Trudy shook her wavy blonde hair, "I don't know honey," she answered. "Why haven't you told me where you live?" She asked.

"Does that make a difference? You don't have to know where I live for me to stop by the smoothie shop or pick you up at your place," he related.

"You must live in a homeless shelter or at the Salvation Army," she said sadly.

"You have seen where I work. I drive an old car. You must know that I am not well-off, but I am not a tramp either," he said. "Okay, I will drive you by my place and then take you home," he offered.

Arthur shut the car door after Trudy had climbed into his old Ford parked outside the diner. The car drove past the beat-up strip malls of West Market Street. After a few miles it turned toward the brick buildings of downtown Greenville. They passed several low-income apartments where college students lived and then entered the downtown area. After three blocks of abandoned businesses, the car turned right onto South Roan Street.

As the drive continued, Trudy noticed that the surroundings became even more depressed. Traveling south on South Roan Street, Arthur slowed to allow a shabby man and woman cross the street. The car then climbed a hill as it exited the city and entered the county going south toward the small farms that comprised the countryside. A few miles into the county the car turned left onto the graveled drive of a trailer park. A rusted sign at the entrance to the trailer park read: "South Side Park." Soon Arthur pulled up to his trailer, bathed in the harsh white light of the lamp on the pine utility pole. The woman's heart sank as she saw the condition in which Arthur lived.

"Quietly putting her hand on his shoulder as they sat in the car out-

43.

side the trailer she then said, "you can take me home now, Arthur."

It was the evening after Arthur had taken Trudy to look at his trailer. "I can't worry if she doesn't like the trailer," he thought. "I am not rich and she knows it," he thought as he was sweeping up in the corner of Zack's about eight o'clock.

The supper crowd had left and Zack's was quiet. At once, the front door swung open. Trudy walked in with a worried look on her face. Seeing Arthur in the corner, Trudy looked down avoiding his gaze. She then walked briskly toward the office and entered, closing the door behind her.

"Who is that talking to Sam?" The cashier asked as she walked over and stood in front of Arthur.

"How do I know?" The embarrassed second shift supervisor mumbled. The door to the office was thin, and Arthur could hear Trudy's excited voice inside.

"I bet Sam has heard it all by now," Arthur thought. "Please don't get me fired Trudy," he whispered under his breath. Then, the door opened and just as suddenly as she had appeared Trudy exited the front door of Zack's.

Sam was sixty-five years old and had worked at Zack's since before the time that Arthur first walked in and applied for a job. Sam had been married for thirty-five years and he had three grown children. Years of Zack's Chicken had taken its toll on Sam's health. He had grown overweight, lost most of his hair and he had high blood pressure. But if there was anyone in Greenville who knew Arthur, it was Sam. To some degree, Arthur and Sam had been friends. In the seventeen years Arthur had worked for Sam they had never exchanged a harsh word. This was because, as the cashiers and cooks put it, Arthur was spineless and would not stand up to Sam.

44.

If Arthur had a problem with an employee on the second shift, he just did the work himself.

"I am not gonna get anyone fired," he told himself once. "Somebody else can to the dirty work," he thought. There had been employees let go, but they had been so bad even Arthur could not hide their faults from Sam.

After Trudy left that night, Sam came out of his office looking angry. He walked up to Arthur, who stood silently holding the broom he had used to sweep up. Confronting Arthur, Sam broke into a wide smile.

"Art, don't you let this little lady get away-I am tellin you," he said in a loud voice so all the employees could hear. "You gotta little spitfire girl fer a friend," Sam said. "Listen Art, you take the rest of the night off. I will close for you," he said and then walked back into his office.

It had been three weeks since Trudy had her talk with Sam at Zack's Chicken. She had not seen Arthur in the interim. Three Saturday nights had passed without his visit. It was late after Trudy had gotten off work. The phone rang and Trudy picked up.

"I think you scared your man off," Elena said over the phone.

"I don't know, Elena, I was just trying to help," Trudy replied.

"Men don't want that kind of help, honey," came over the phone.

"Maybe I ought to call and see how he is feeling. What do you think?" The smoothie clerk asked.

"You think he might have found some other girl?" Elena asked.

45.

"I can find out honey. It won't be that hard," Trudy said.

"Really? You think a man is gonna tell you if he is two-timing you?" the grocery store clerk said sarcastically.

"I have a plan," Trudy said. "I will let you know what I find out," she concluded.

During the three weeks that Trudy had wondered, alone in her shop, what had happened to Arthur, he had been busy at work. Two of the servers and the senior cook had quit.

"How are they going to find a better place to work?" Arthur asked Sam.

"There ain't no good places to work. All the places in this town are bad, and you know that as well as I," Sam told his long time friend.

"The owner of this place, that ol man is mean as a mule," Sam confessed to Arthur.

While he cleaned the tables, cooked the biscuits and rang up the orders, Arthur had been thinking about his woman friend. From morning until night he could see her supple frame, with her white skin and charming smile present in his memory. As he closed in the evenings, he imagined that the blonde woman with the black eyebrows was waiting for him in her car in the parking lot of Zack's. Once off work, he imagined that he and Trudy would sit together in her car and talk until they both had to go home.

"How is Trudy doin?" Sam asked Arthur one night.

"Hadn't been by to see her since she was here," Arthur told his boss.

Sam's eyes widened. "Whut is wrong with you brother?" Sam

asked abruptly. "You git yerself over and see her, before it's too late," he told his friend.

Arthur did not need any further prodding. After work that night, he walked through the door of Trudy's shop. There was another male in the shop. He was at the counter talking to Trudy. Arthur felt his back and neck stiffen. Walking to his table, he tried to get a look at the man. The customer was older, maybe fifty years old or so. He was well dressed and very muscular and trim. Arthur sat down at the table and waited.

"I should have come by before now," he grumbled.

It seemed like at least thirty minutes before "Mr. Conviviality" left, Arthur looked over and did not see Trudy.

"Did she leave with the older man?" He wondered. He stood up and looked around. Then he started to leave.

"Where do you think you are goin, honey?" he heard Trudy shout from the rear of the work area. Without answering, Arthur returned to his seat at the table and sat down. Soon, Trudy appeared from the back of the shop, walked over and sat down beside him.

"Trudy, I am sorry I haven't stopped by sooner, but Sam is a slave-driver," Arthur said quickly.

"That is okay, honey...Malcolm has been stopping by to take up for you," Trudy said and her lips curled into a smile.

"So Malcolm is the old guy you were talking to....Is that it?" Arthur said, trying to suppress the irritation in his voice. Arthur then no-ticed that his friend was wearing a low-cut, cherry colored blouse. His eyes were attracted by the soft whiteness of Trudy's throat and neck and the covered shapes of her bosom. Trudy then tossed her hair with her head. The pretty blonde locks settled back down around her cheeks.

47.

"Penny for your thoughts," she said knowingly.

"Why don't I pick you up at your place Friday night and we can go see a movie?" He suggested.

"Okay, hun," she said, "as long as you are not too busy."

The two single people then caught up on three weeks of not seeing one another. After Arthur left, Trudy locked up the shop and walked to her car.

"I got him right where I want him," she thought with satisfaction.

"Is there another girl, honey?...Tell me everything," Elena said loudly as she took a bite from a double decker hamburger. It was two p.m. and Trudy and Elena sat at the diner having lunch.

"Arthur said, he's been busy...with work...that is what he said honey," Trudy replied.

"Sure," Elena then put her hand on Trudy's arm.

"No, Elena, I think Arthur is different from other guys," and Trudy adopted a serious look. "And anyway, honey, even if he did wander a bit, he is back in my pocket," the blonde woman said.

"So when is he picking you up?" Elena said in a low tone.

"This Friday night; we are going to the cinema," her friend replied.

Then Trudy looked down at her plate and frowned. "I gotta get rid of Malcolm," she said. "I think he is gonna be a problem for me," she continued. "He keeps coming by three times a week, and he hangs around the shop for ever," she said.

"Double trouble, honey...At his age there is either a wife somewhere or he has been divorced three times," Elena related.

"I know Trudy, tell Malcolm you don't care for men the age of your father," Elena said.

"I have to do something...This thing with him has been going on too long," Trudy confessed.

49.
Part Three

Five years passed and Trudy and Arthur were still together. Trudy had become the assistant manager of the smoothie shop on North Roan Street. Sam had retired and Arthur had taken over as general manager of Zack's Chicken. Enough time had passed for Arthur to buy a new double-wide trailer, but he still lived in South Side Park on South Roan Street. Trudy had upgraded to a more spacious apartment on the north side of Greenville.

"How is he?" Elena asked Trudy.

It was ten o'clock p.m. at the Market Street Diner and the two friends sat before colas and a basket of curly fries.

"What do you mean?" Trudy asked. "Arthur is okay. He still works at Zack's Chicken," she answered in confusion.

"No, I mean how is he at it?" Elena said firmly looking straight into Trudy's eyes.

"You mean at kissing?" Trudy asked.

"What else do you think I mean, honey? Of course...I mean kissing," Elena repeated. "He has kissed you, honey, hasn't he? After all, how long have you two been together?" She asked Trudy.

"Well, honey, there was no kissing for the first two years," the smoothie clerk confessed.

"You must be kidding," Elena blurted out.

"He just wouldn't try..." Trudy said and then her voice trailed off. She looked down into the basket of fries and fell silent.

"But is it good?" Her companion persisted.

"It's good, honey. I tell you, when he bends down to kiss me,

50.

I barely feel his lips touching mine," Trudy said.

Elena sat straight up and thought for a minute. "Oh, honey...Gentle is what makes a real man...Don't you agree?" She asked.

"Yes, but Elena, haven't you been kissed?" Trudy asked, looking across the table at her friend.

"Well, I have told you before about my marriage," Elena's voice sounded raspy. "What Ed did was not what I would call a real kiss. I would rather call his kiss an attack upon decency," Elena said despondently. She then continued..."Well, honey...I won't ask you any think else between you and Arthur. If there is anything else, better keep it private," she said. "Some things are not the business of even your best girlfriend," she said flatly.

"Your friend Beth has someone, hasn't she?" Trudy asked Elena.

"Beth has Wayne," Elena said in an irritated tone of voice. "You know, Trudy...Wayne is married, but Beth hangs around him like a ship's anchor," she said. "I told Beth when this thing with Wayne started that she was wasting her time," Elena said. "You know Beth thinks that Wayne really loves her. When she told me this, I couldn't believe my ears...This is so much non-sense," Elena said.

"Maybe Elena, it's Beth that loves Wayne," Trudy said knowingly.

After the first year of their relationship, with still a year to go before the first kiss between Trudy and Arthur, they had been attending a bowling league on Sunday afternoons. Arthur had first introduced the idea one night while they were having dinner together at Cafe Lola's. Trudy had ordered a Caesar salad and tuna on a croissant. Although fancy food was not a favorite with the chicken cook, Arthur sat that night before a cheese tort. Arthur had been embarrassed when his girlfriend had told him she wanted to go to Cafe Lola's.

51.

"That is the place for rich old ladies to have lunch," he had told her.

"Do I have to ask you twice?" Trudy said looking defiantly at him.

"I tell you what Trudy, I will take you to Cafe Lola's anytime you want if you will go bowling with me at Holiday Lanes anytime I want," he had stated. "How about it?" He asked her.

"I think I can learn to like this deal, honey," she said with a smile on her face.

It was two p,m. on Sunday at Holiday Lanes. Arthur had been struggling with his bowling game on this day.

"Ugh, another gutter ball," he complained as he released his ball only to find it quickly end up on the side of the bowling lane.

Trudy's game was graceful. She skipped up the lane and skillfully released her ball.

"A spare," she shouted as she returned from releasing her ball.

Arthur had the opportunity to notice how her skimpy yellow shorts gripped her hips and thighs.

"She is really in good shape," he remarked under his breath as she threw the second ball to knock down the spare.

Sitting back down beside her boyfriend, Trudy said, "I think I am gonna buy my own pink bowling ball."

Arthur looked over at her cheerful face. "At my level, I better stay with the worn, rental balls here at Holiday Plaza," he said. "If I came up with the cash to buy a nice bowling ball, it would be a waste," he complained.

Arthur went to the grill for pizza and soda. After he returned, Trudy picked up a piece of pizza and fed it to her boyfriend.

"This is the best part of being here at Holiday Lanes," he said as he wiped tomato sauce from his face.

"A girl can't eat too much of the pizza and still keep her figure, honey," Trudy said looking over at him.

"I don't see much danger of that happenin Trudy," Arthur said. "Here Trudy, I guess I will eat the rest," and Arthur quickly made the rest of the pizza disappear.

It was a hot Sunday afternoon when the pair left Holiday Lanes. As the old sedan started, it began making a clanking noise and the front end shook.

"Honey, what is wrong with this thing?" Trudy asked in alarm.

"Don't worry, it will take us where we are going," Arthur promised.

The car pulled out onto Broyles Avenue and the driver turned right onto North Roan Street. Trudy lived about three miles away in an apartment in the county. In two minutes, Arthur made a right turn onto the county road. Suddenly, the car lost power and steam emanated from under the hood. The car rolled ahead slowly and then stopped.

"I told you last year, Arthur, that this thing was not going to last," Trudy said in a loud voice. "Who was it who didn't listen to his girlfriend's advice?" She demanded.

"I'll get you home and worry about this piece of junk later. A good customer at work owns "Reliable Cab," he said as he pulled out his cell phone and began dialing a number.

53.
Arthur and Trudy sat in the overheated car waiting for Arthur's
friend, Mel and his "Reliable Cab."

Arthur and Trudy sat in the car waiting for Arthur's friend, Mel. The
sun shining through the windshield hurt the eyes of the couple.

Arthur reflected, "I know Trudy is much smarter that I am. How
does she put up with me?" He asked himself.

As if she had read his mind, Trudy leaned over and hugged him,
"don't worry about the car Arthur, it's the driver of the car I can't let
go," she said.

It secretly pleased Trudy so see that her boyfriend was not perfect
and invincible. Mel picked up Trudy in his cab and they left for her
apartment. Arthur dialed an one eight-hundred number for the
Triple B Car Club. A recorded voice came to the line and then the
line went dead.

"Triple B is worthless," he thought. "I am gonna cancel those jerks
at Triple B," he promised himself.

The county road where Arthur's car was stalled was within walking distance of Kroger on Sunset Drive. Sam's oldest son was the
assistant manager at Kroger. Arthur got out of his car and began
walking back toward the outskirts of Greenville. The county road
was narrow and hilly. The pavement radiated the afternoon heat
into Arthur's face as he trudged toward the Kroger store. Arthur
was thin and he did not work out as Trudy did. He was not physi-
cally strong.

"I don't need to exercise," he told himself once. "All I need is to get

54.

through a twelve-hour shift and then make it to a couch," he had
believed.

Now, as the walk toward Kroger became dreary and his feet ached,
he heard a car pull up behind him and honk its horn. He turned
his head to face the intruder only to see Trudy sitting in the driver's
seat. She pulled her car into the lane beside him and motioned him
into the car. She then drove to the Brown's Mill Towing Company
where Arthur arranged to have his car towed to the garage on Bristol Highway.

"Can a pretty lady take me home?" He then asked Trudy after the
tow truck had left with his car.

"You read my mind, honey," she said.

"You mean his car died right there in the middle of the county
road?" Elena said with exasperation.

It was late at night and the two friends were at the Market Street
Diner. Elena put a beef taco into her mouth and began chewing.
Across the table from her Trudy took a long drink of her sweet tea.

"I don't know if Arthur can afford a new car right now, you know he
just bought that double-wide trailer," she said.

"Which do you like better honey, this hard-shell taco of the soft-shell
kind?" Elena asked.

"Well, the soft-shell kind is easier on my teeth," Trudy said. "Those
pieces of hard-shell keep getting stuck between my teeth," she said
and she held out her hand holding a soft-shell chicken taco.

55.
"You know, Trudy," Elena announced, "Sanchez Grocer sells all the ingredients for the tacos and burritos here at the diner," she said with satisfaction. ""How is Arthur's work going, Trudy, is he happy?" Elena asked her friend.

"Well Elena, he might as well be happy, it took him twenty-three years to make manager," Trudy said. "And I can tell you one thing for sure, honey: he is crazy about your's truly," Trudy said as she looked over Elena's shoulder into the far corner of the diner.

On the television hanging from the ceiling in the corner was a news item about a Greenville doctor who had been sentenced to fifteen years in prison.

"Listen to this Elena: this doctor who had a big pain clinic is going up the river for fifteen years," Trudy said with excitement. "The big shot doctor was selling pain pill subscriptions by the dozen," she said.

"My aunt was addicted to oxycodone, Trudy, but I don't know who gave it to her," Elena said.

"Wasn't your Ed into drugs, honey?" Trudy asked.

"Well, Ed didn't get his fix from a doctor, he got it from the local pusher," Elena said firmly.

"This doctor on the news, he was just another kind of pusher, if you ask me," her friend said.

"Greenville is a nice town, honey, but we have plenty of people here with big problems," Elena concluded.

"If Greenville weren't such a nice town, Elena, folks like you and my Arthur wouldn't be living here," Trudy said. "Tell your boss, Pablo, that the salsa he sells the diner is the best," she finished.

After Elena left the diner, Trudy picked up her purse and walked out to her car. "I am gonna stop by and see my one-and-only," she thought as she drove down West Market Street.

Gwyneth worked in the kitchen at Zack's. She was nineteen years old and had moved out on her own a few months before. Earlier, she had made rent by working the cash register nights at the Road Runner Market. In the evenings at Road Runner, she had felt un-safe as a solo female with mostly older males frequenting the store. Shoplifting had been a problem and the police had told her that they refused to prosecute theft-there was just too much of it in Green-ville. At Zack's as a kitchen worker, Gwyneth was not exposed to the public. She was small in stature and wore mannish clothes. Her skin was very fair and her hair was cut short on the sides of her head with long hair on the top gathered together by a clasp. When Arthur interviewed Gwyneth he knew that she needed his help.

When Trudy entered Zack's after talking to Elena at the West Mar-ket Diner she looked around and did not see Arthur. There were three couples finishing their meals and a young man was sweeping up. She entered the manager's office. Arthur sat behind his old desk having a meeting with Gwyneth.

"Is this private, honey?" Trudy asked, looking from her boyfriend to the young woman..

"Not at all Trudy, have a seat beside Gwyneth," Arthur said.

It was ten o'clock, one hour before closing, this Monday night. Gwyneth looked upset and there were tear stains down her cheeks. As Trudy sat down, the young woman fell silent.

Arthur spoke up, "Gwyn here has been on her own just a few months living by herself in a walk-up flat downtown," he said. He looked at his employee and continued, "this week the police raided

57.

the apartment next to hers and discovered a meth lab," he continued.

"Mr. Reagan, sir, there was a loud noise comin frum their rooms
every night," Gwyneth said staring down at the floor in front of her
chair. "I cain't go on livin there," she said quietly and then she
turned and glanced at Trudy.

"Honey, my friend, Elena, is looking for a room-mate. How do you
feel about cats? Elena has an older cat, Otis," Trudy conveyed.

"Cats are okay. I just didn't get along with my mother and sister. I
swear I will keep my mouth shut around your friend if she will take
me in," Gwyneth pleaded.

"Okay, honey, let me talk to her tomorrow," Trudy finished.

"The chicken is waiting for the fryer, Gwyn. That is all for now," Arthur concluded.

Three days later it was Gwyneth's night off. As usual, she sat in her
apartment alone. It was now eight o'clock and she had just finished
washing and drying the plastic dishes that she had purchased at
Target.

"Cheap is key," she had explained to a friend to justify her frequent
trips to Target. Roach traps had been placed in the corners of the
efficiency walk-up flat. She slept on a sleeper-couch that she had
bought at Good-Will on Bristol Highway. For warmth there were
cheap, synthetic blankets and under them were cotton sheets and
a cotton pillow case protected the old feather pillow. No matter
how many roach traps Gwyneth placed in the rooms, roaches were
everywhere.

"Where do these bugs come from?" She had asked herself soon
after she had moved in. "I don't keep food laying around," she had
thought with frustration. "I swear, I don't know how they stay alive,"

58.
she exclaimed one night.

There was a loud rap upon the wooden front door.

The nineteen-year-old peered through the small round piece of glass in the middle of the door. There was tall, forty-something woman with blue hair pulled back on her head into a bun.

"She looks like she lives like me," Gwyneth thought as she unfastened the security chair and slowly opened the door.

"I am Trudy's friend, Elena," the woman said while peering around the door at Gwyneth. The door opened widely and Gwyneth stood before Elena.

"Come on in, Trudy tol me all about you," Gwyneth said as Elena walked into the middle of the room.

"We women have got to stick together, honey," Elena said to Gwyneth. "Trudy said that you need help and Trudy's boyfriend, Arthur, told me that you are reliable," Elena conveyed.

"Look Elena, I need to get outa here right now," the young woman explained. "Except for my sleeper couch, everything I have will fit into my car," she said. "I kin have friends move the couch into your place in a day or two," Gwyneth said.

"Are you in some kinda trouble?" Elena asked.

"Trouble follows me where-ever I go, Elena," Gwyneth explained. "My dad, mom and my sister are all big trouble," Gwyneth said in a hoarse voice.

"I know trouble," the forty-year old said. My dad is a Missionary Baptist minister, and he thinks I need to spend most of my life in church, and the rest of it praying and reading the Bible," Elena explained with a frown.

59.
Within two hours Gwyneth lay on a sheet on the floor of Elena's apartment. A solitary blanket lay on top of her. Her worried head rested on a feather pillow. She slept soundly that night.

"That Gwyneth is not completely socialized," Elena complained one night as she sat with Trudy at the diner about one week later.

"What exactly does that mean, honey?" Trudy asked.

"She seems temperamental and out-of-sorts all of the time," Elena continued.

"You need to put her on a reward system," Trudy said and then continued: "tell her she will get points off her share of the rent if she helps around the apartment," Trudy said with a serious look on her face.

"I can give her five points for doing the dishes and ten points for not arguing," Elena said.

"Have you ever lived with another girl?" Trudy asked.

"Not until now, but I have heard that most girls are dirty and have filthy mouths," Elena said. "Even like that, I would take Gwyneth over my ex, Ed, anytime," Elena said.

"See there, honey...It can't be that bad. Anyway, she needs help getting on her feet," Trudy said.

"My problem when I moved out was not getting on my feet; it was cutting down on all the visits from my mother," Elena said. "From what Gwyneth tells me, she won't have any problem with her family coming over: they are toxic and she is glad to be rid of them," Elena said with finality.

Arthur sat at the smoothie shop the next Saturday night sipping his

60.
weekly Mango Magic smoothie.

"Elena told me, honey, that Gwyneth is great help with the monthly rent," Trudy mentioned as she washed some plastic tumblers.

"That is good to know, Trudy, because I cannot afford to look for another cook. This girl is a real worker," Arthur replied. He then turned and looked at his girlfriend. "Trudy is unusually pretty to-night," he thought.

Arthur then fell silent and his eyes wandered over Trudy's perky face, wavy hair and her firm, well-molded body as she worked. The female form had the effect of creating a warm feeling in him. Although the day at Zack's had been hectic, he felt happy at this moment. All the tenseness soon flowed out of his body.

"I don't need therapy; I just need her," he reflected. "What will hap-pen to me if Trudy finds another man that she likes more than me?" He worried.

"I am just not going to think about losing her. I better make darned sure I keep her happy," he concluded.

61.

62.
Elena in Two Parts

63.
Part One

Elena was now forty-one years old. It had been a decade or more since Beth and Wayne had become chummy, despite the steady objections from Elena. In the meantime, Beth and Wayne had maintained what Beth would term "a respectable friendship." Elena suspected that something scandalous was happening between the two, but she could never uncover definite proof of this.

"Beth cannot fool me," Elena said, and she frowned as she stacked cans of refried beans on the shelves of Sanchez Grocery. "I doubt whether Beth or Wayne have any morals," she reflected.

Otis was now an elderly cat. His gait was stiff and he now had difficulty jumping onto Elena's bed. Elena maintained the same apartment, and a nineteen-year old girl, Gwyneth, had moved in and become Elena's room-mate. At seven o'clock Elena finished stocking the shelves and walked to the front of the store. Night had fallen, but the bright lights of the utility poles in the parking lot shone through the front windows of the small store. Pablo's wife, Rosa, was beginning to close up for the night.

"Honey, go straight you home, not go downtown," Rosa advised in a motherly tone of voice.

"Don't worry, Rosa, I have not been downtown in Greenville since I was in high school," the clerk replied.

Elena had always been a model of probity. Because of that, there had not been much excitement in her world. Her life revolved around work and sitting in her apartment. She did have friends: she had Beth despite her distaste of Beth's behavior with Wayne, and she had Trudy who was a more serious woman than Beth. Trudy's boyfriend, Arthur, had put Elena in contact with Gwyneth-her room-mate.

64.

Later that night back in her apartment, Elena picked up her phone and dialed a number.

"Girl, I haven't heard from you in a month," Beth answered loudly over the line.

"I have been busy, Beth, you know how that is," Elena said in response. "How are things with Wayne?" She asked in anticipation.

"Oh, Elena, he is such a big baby," Beth said eagerly.

"How is that honey? The man must be seventy-five by now," Elena said in an unfriendly tone. "Doesn't he ever talk about Shelley with you, honey?" The clerk asked.

"If he wanted to talk about her, he is welcome," Beth said. "I have told him this over and over," she said.

"What else have you told him, Beth?" Elena demanded.

"You know, Elena, last week I met him at the diner at ten o'clock," Beth said and continued, "he was so upset I had to settle his nerves."

"And what were you wearing, honey? I hope you have stopped wearing the low-cut polka dot blouse," Elena said sharply.

"Oh, no, I would never throw that precious blouse away. It gives me such a free and feminine rush just to show off to him," Beth said.

"That is in poor taste," Elena thought to herself and she then spoke, "you can't afford to get him going, Beth, he might not know how to stop. What do you think you are doing honey?" Elena warned.

"I don't know, Elena, flirting is so much fun, and honey it is all completely innocent," Beth promised. "Well, I have to go know, bye," and Elena hung up the telephone

65.
receiver.

As Elena hung up the phone, she could see in her mind's eye, Beth escorting Wayne into her apartment. Elena grimaced to herself and then could not suppress a feeling of jealousy. Although Elena was a shy person, and quiet in groups, she was a woman of strong emotion.

"Who was that on the phone, Elena?" Gwyneth asked from across the room.

"Just a friend honey," Elena said.

When Elena was jealous, and this was often, her stomach would tighten and she would feel like her body was tied in knots. Elena walked to the bathroom and opened the door to the medicine cabinet. She took out two Valiums and swallowed them down with a glass of tepid water from the tap. In the ten years that Beth and Wayne had been pursuing their friendship, Elena had been learning things about Wayne. She knew where he lived, the type of car that he drove, and she had a general grasp of his usual weekly activities. Beth was such a talker it had not been difficult for the clerk to put together the details of Wayne's life. Shelley, Elena had discovered, was a customer of Sanchez Grocery.

"I doubt the poor woman knows anything about Beth," she had thought during the times she saw Shelley shopping at Sanchez Grocery.

In the ten years since Wayne had agreed to become Beth's friend, Beth's life had been transformed. Before Wayne, she had struggled to get up each morning. Although Beth had always been attractive and outgoing, she was now more meticulous about her appearance.

"I know how to please Wayne. I am gonna give him a real reason to look at me," she had promised herself from the outset.

66.

Over her fifty years of life, Beth had always had advantages over other women regarding her feminine endowments. Now she would be sure not to lose the special look in Wayne's eyes when they sat together at the diner. She had consulted her doctor on health-conscious diets. Except for her weekly meal with Wayne, she now rarely ate meat and focused rather on whole wheat bread, fresh fruit and vegetables. Although on the scales Beth learned that she had lost eight pounds, in Wayne's eyes she had always been very attractive. When the Greenville sun rose in the morning, Beth did her exercises.

Gwyneth turned her key in the lock to Elena's apartment and entered.

"This place is pig sty," she said to herself.

Otis approached her and began to rub against her leg. She reached down, patted him on the back, and then pushed him away. "I never liked Otis, cats are too selfish," she thought.

Her sleeper couch was in the corner of the main room with the blankets in disorder.

"Why make things up when they just get messed up again so soon?" She reflected.

She pushed the rumpled blanket on the couch down and closed the seat of the sleeper couch over it. As a result the couch seats angled up at the front of the cushions and did not lay flat.

"I better get things straightened up before the old woman gets home," she thought.

She walked to the sink in the kitchenette and turned on the hot water. The pipes made a whining noise and the water was slightly orange with rust from the pipes. She picked up a bottle of dish washing soap and squirted the bright green soap over a pile of gray

67.
dishes she had purchased at Target.

As Gwyneth sat down on her sofa after finishing the dishes, the door to the apartment swung open.

"I have had it with Beth," Elena fumed as she walked in.

"What is up now?" Gwyneth complained.

"Wayne's wife Shelley came by the store today. She is so clueless," Elena said fiercely.

"Isn't this Beth's business and not yours?" The ill-tempered Gwyneth offered back.

"How can this Wayne carry on with Beth, while Shelley is in such poor health?" The forty-one year old asked her room-mate.

"You are terminally jealous, honey," the nineteen year old said.

"You got to be kidding, honey," Elena said. "I don't need any boy trouble. I had that with Ed," she said.

"Well, honey, I am lookin for just the kind of problem that your friend Beth has. I wouldn't mind it a bit," Gwyneth said and she stood up facing Elena.

"You'll have to find a wonder man on your own honey. You are in for a long wait," Elena said.

At this point, Gwyneth's temper rose from five-out-of-ten to ten-out-of-ten.

"I better shut up right now or I might get throwed out," she reflected as she retreated toward the bathroom and shut the door behind her.

Elena looked at the rear side of Gwyneth as the girl made for the bathroom.

68.

"Now I am in for it," Elena thought. "Gwyneth won't talk to me for a week," she grumbled.

Elena then cooked her dinner and sat in her stuffed chair to eat it alone. After two hours, she ambled back to her bedroom and climbed into bed. As she drifted off to sleep, Gwyneth was still in the bathroom with the door closed and locked. Gwyneth sat on the toilet and her mind wandered back to high school and her boyfriend Teddy.

"Why did I have to fall in love with Teddy?" She asked herself. "I should have played the field and had fun. Being serious about someone is sheer misery," she reflected.

Teddy had been Gwyneth's first, and even now, only boyfriend. In high school they had met in English class where Gwyneth excelled and Teddy nearly flunked. She had been Teddy's tutor after hours at the request of their teacher-a wavy headed and plump thirty-six year old woman. Teddy's only interest had been music, and after his split from Gwyneth and graduation from school, he worked as a disc jockey in Greenville. The romance had lasted all of four months, after which Gwyneth had noticed her man flirting with other girls in class. Not one to give up easily, she had held on until finally he dumped her.

"Everyone in school knows what Teddy did to you, Gwyn," her friend Tracy had told her one day as they rode home on the school bus.

It didn't seem to matter to Gwyneth that she had been treated bad-ly, she could not shake her feelings for him. Even now, four years later, she had not even considered dating.

"That Gwyneth has got to start talking sometime," Elena com-plained to Trudy. "Elena, Gwyneth has been through much. After all, she is only

69.
nineteen and her people threw her out," Trudy explained.

"But she is so ignorant," Elena became emphatic. "She says that
she wants the same kind of trouble that Beth is making for herself.
I doubt the girl has ever had a relationship with a man. Have you
seen her appearance?" Elena asked.

"This crazy look of hers, honey...This is simply rebellion," Trudy
advised. "I think, if she will let me fix her up, some guy would take
a long look in her direction," Trudy said.

"Well, you can try if you want. The girl will not listen to me," Elena
said.

Trudy became silent and began to reflect on Gwyneth's looks.

"She is petite...Very good, Trudy thought. "Growing out that horrible hair style would do wonders," she thought. "Nice clothes would
help, once she has saved some money. I will tell Arthur to drop
some hints her way at work," she concluded. "I bet a nineteen year
old girl will listen to what Arthur says," Trudy concluded.

"That little Gwyneth is a great worker," Arthur thought as he sat in
his office at Sam's old desk. He had a copy of a fashion magazine
in his lap.

"Trudy is right, Gwyneth could use some sprucing up," he reflected.

He walked to the open door of his office and motioned Janice
inside. Janice walked in. She was twenty-five with a blonde page-
boy haircut, close-fitting athletic style clothing and bright pink lipstick.

"Look at this picture," he said as he gave the magazine to Janice.
"Our new cook could use some advice on appearance," he said
looking straight at the young woman.

"Well, I think she is getting that message from the male waiters,"

70.
Janice replied.

"Lay this on one of the stove tops for me while Gwyneth is watching you," Arthur suggested.

Janice picked up the magazine and walked back to the front counter.

The nineteen year old had not dated for four years, but she did have eyes that could see and a brain that could think. She had noticed how Danny, one of the waiters, followed Janice around.

"That Janice is so smug," Gwyneth thought the night the blonde walked up to her and placed the fashion magazine on the counter before her. "These Greenville guys don't know the kind of girl that Janice really is," the cook thought to herself.

Gwyneth picked up the magazine and thumbed through its pages.

A few days later Elena sat in her stuffed chair in her apartment. It was three o'clock on a Saturday afternoon. She had slept until one o'clock and Gwyneth had been out for hours. There had only been fleeting conversations between the two women since their fight over Beth's friendship with Wayne.

"Doesn't Beth know that a married man like Wayne is double trouble," Elena thought as she took up her crochet hook and began to work the yarn. She had been making a yellow sweater for herself to wear later when the weather was cool. It was August at this time. The doorknob to her apartment began to turn with a creaking sound and Gwyneth appeared looking around the room anxiously.

"I don't know why the girl wears such an ugly hair style," Elena thought as she looked Gwyneth over.

For the first time since she had moved in, her room-mate was not wearing a pair of faded baggy jeans. She had on a short, black nylon skirt. Gwyneth walked across the room and put a bag of sun-

71.

dries on her folded up sleeper couch.

"The sweater looks nice Elena," she said as she spied the piece of clothing in progress. Elena looked at her with fixed attention.

"Gwyneth has killer legs," she thought as her mind raced onward.

Gwyneth was small in stature, with rounded calves and well-molded thighs.

"That skirt is not my type," Elena thought and then made a judgment call. "I would not let any of the Greenville men see me with that much pale skin below my skirt," she frowned to herself.

Gwyneth sat down on the cushions of her couch and shook off her two sandals. Then she began to paint her little toenails bright red as she propped her shapely legs onto the seat of a nearby wicker chair.

"If I were a man sitting here, there wouldn't be much that I couldn't see," the forty-one year old woman reflected. "How are things at work, honey?" Elena asked. "Is Arthur treating you okay?" She continued.

"Oh, he is great," Gwyneth said with emphasis. "Some of the boy employees don't know a shameless tart when she sashays herself around," the nineteen year old offered.

"What do you mean?" Her room-mate blurted out.

"It's that Janice, Elena. She has Danny, Joe and Phillip all doing her work," Gwyneth said. ""The hussy says jump and all the men jump" she said. "I am gonna give that Janice sum competition," she concluded.

Gwyneth stood up from the couch once her toenails were painted and walked over to a long mirror on legs in the corner of the room. She looked intently at her face in the mirror and began smoothing

72.

her misshapen hair around.

Two weeks later in the evening, Elena and Gwyneth sat in Elena's apartment listening to WDXR Radio 6, Greenville. Elena was in her stuffed chair crocheting and Gwyneth lay back on the sleeper couch with her head propped against one of the arms of the couch. WDXR Radio 6 was the only station in Greenville that wasn't country. Now that they were speaking to one another, the two women found that they shared a common taste in popular music. "Blue Bayou" was playing sung by a performer named Roy Orbison, now long dead.

Suddenly, Gwyneth sat upright as the disc jockey began his chatter and walked over and switched the radio off.

"What is wrong with you honey?...That's Teddy, the best disc jockey in Greenville," Elena said in a loud voice. "Are you thinking of that horrible girl, Janice, at Zack's Chicken who has all the men running after her?" Elena asked.

"It...It's the men in Greenville, Elena...I haven't met a one of them that knows a high-value girl when he meets her," Gwyneth said.

"Honey, the men around here are all dirt bags...You have my word on it," Elena confirmed.

Elena had noticed a subtle shake in Gwyneth's voice as she complained about Greenville men.

"I thought the only feelings she has are anger and boredom," the forty-one year old thought to herself.

"What kind of man trouble have you had honey? All of us women can talk about that," Elena cautiously said.

"I...I can't talk about it right now, Elena," Gwyneth mumbled as she walked over to the counter near the sink and began putting the washed dinner dishes away.

73.

"Finding someone good for you isn't easy honey," Elena said.

"You better be like me; just give up and forget about happiness,"
and Elena's body shuddered as she said this.

74.
Part Two

A sudden transformation had occurred at Zack's Chicken after Gwyneth declared war on Janice. One Tuesday afternoon, the usually frumpy and unpopular chicken cook arrived at starting time in the short, black nylon dress that had shocked Elena so much. Every man in the restaurant had a full view of Gwyneth's legs with skin of pure white. Gwyneth's family, although dysfunctional in nature, was peopled by females of jet-black hair and flawless, pale complexions. Gwyneth did not have to shave her legs. They were naturally smooth. Not only did the young girl display her legs, but her midriff was gripped by a tight-fitting blue blouse that accentuated every curve from her narrow waist to her supple neck. Danny and the other male staff could not believe the change in a girl they were accustomed to ignore. Like every woman, Gwyneth could see the effect she had on these men without revealing that she knew all that was going on in their minds.

Later in the evening, Joe, a lanky blonde waiter, approached the hot burners of the stove as the cooking was proceeding.

"Gwyneth...Could I have a moment of your time?" He said quietly.

Gwyneth turned and fixed her blue eyes on him. Joe felt a sudden weakening of his resolve.

"Uh, all the customers tonight say...Are a'sayin that yer cookin is sumthin special," he stammered.

As Joe stood there before her, his eyes roamed nervously about Gwyneth's figure. The cook stopped and held up one arm, signaling an "A Okay" with her tapered fingers with her small nails painted bright yellow.

From the back of Zack's, Joe heard Janice shout: "Joe, table three is outa iced tea...You hear me?" She said.

Joe turned around and retreated toward one of the tables where

75.

Danny and Phillip stood.

"Wow...Brother man...I can't believe how good our Gwyneth looks," Danny said to Joe.

"You got it...This young thing is sumthin else," Joe answered with emphasis.

"Listen Joe, don't you and Danny get too interested in Gwyneth. You two have got girlfriends. I am the poor soul who is woman-less," Phillip said.

As Phillip finished giving his advice to his two friends, Janice approached their table and threw a wet dishrag onto its top.

"What're you two think Arthur is paying you for?" There are two tables with customers waiting to give their orders," she said.

Phillip, Danny and Joe were well acquainted with the feisty Janice. Joe looked up and his gaze met the stare of Janice's green eyes. The three men made a hasty exit for the opposite side of the dining room. Joe and Danny grabbed menus and hurried to the waiting tables. As closing time approached, Arthur gave Gwyneth approval to leave, and Joe approached Janice at the door.

"You look pretty tonight, Janice," he grinned.

"That's right honey, and don't you forget how pretty I am!" She snapped.

Soon the lights were turned out and Zack's was empty and closed for the night.

The door to Elena's apartment swung open. Elena felt the draft of cold air enter the apartment from the unheated hall. It was almost eleven p.m. and Gwyneth appeared.

"Short black mini-skirt and too tight blouse," Elena thought to herself.

Back in the kitchenette a pot of tomato soup was steaming. Elena stood up in the middle of the room and loomed over the petite Gwyneth. She gave the nineteen year old a long and serious look. Not wanting to start another fight with her room-mate, Elena left to answer the phone as it began to ring.

"Yes, Beth, she is finally back and honey she is headed for trouble," Elena whispered into the receiver.

In her apartment, Beth was sitting on the side of her unmade bed in the bedroom with the telephone receiver held to one ear.

"She has got to have some fun, Elena," Beth retorted.

"You mean, like you...Running around?" Elena said.

"Elena, stop that this minute...Wayne is a good man. Gwyneth needs someone," Beth answered.

"Beth honey, you know I love you, but there are better things for you in life than a man who is taken," Elena said.

"Taken now...Not taken later, Elena...And in the meantime I am not putting too much pressure on Wayne," Beth said.

"Well, what do you two say to each other the times you sneak around?" Elena asked.

"Change of subject honey...What does Gwyneth say these days about Zack's?" Beth asked.

"For one thing, she says that Janice has it in for her," Elena said.

"Men aren't stupid honey. Arthur won't give that Janice any ear," Beth then said.

77.

"I don't know Beth. Trudy says Janice has Arthur by the nose and leads him around like a puppy," Elena replied.

The next day, both Gwyneth and Janice were dressed for the effect. Janice was wearing green shorts that were very tight fitting and a white, sleeveless blouse with a low-plunging neckline. The golden color of her bare legs and arms was typical of blonde women of Scandinavian origin.

"Danny, can you help me with these trays?" Janice threw an imploring look in his direction.

Danny hurried over and grabbed the stack of plastic trays from her arms.

"Here, let me take those....They are too heavy for you," he said as he took them from her.

Relieved of the trays, Janice bent over in front of him showing off the open throat of her blouse, and she began wiping down the table in front of her with a damp rag. Danny quickly looked away and hurried through the kitchen door, arms full of trays, to the heavy duty dishwasher. As he passed Gwyneth, she was hunched over the stove with her rounded rear and shapely back to him. She had on another mini-dress. This dress was red. He gave her a long sidelong glance and then walked to the back of the kitchen.

After Danny loaded the dishwasher, he pulled out a cigarette for a smoke. Although Arthur had told all of the waiters not to smoke in the kitchen, they knew that he could not see behind the dishwasher. Soon Phillip joined him.

"Take a drag and relax, man," Danny advised his friend.

"I don't know what Janice and Gwyneth are trying to do to us," Phillip said as he pulled out a cigarette. "My poor heart can only take so much stress from these pretty legs and all," he whined.

"You must be crazy," Danny answered. "These kinda women are what us guys are living and praying for," he replied.

Gwyneth had just finished frying a batch of chicken and had been on her way to the freezer for more chicken parts when she over-heard Danny and Phillip.

"Those two guys are such sweethearts," she thought. "They could teach my horrible old Teddy what a good womin is really all about," she reflected. "I need love worse than any girl I know," she thought.

For the rest of the evening, the black-headed cook in the red mini-skirt was happy.

Three weeks later, Gwyneth and Elena were spending a Friday night listening to the radio. In her usual understated style, Elena had taken up her crocheting. Gwyneth lay back on her sleeper couch with her head propped against one end, using the arm of the couch as a cushion for her head.

"Elena, do you think the guys will like me better if I get blue streaks dyed into my hair?" She asked.

"Honey, the guys like you no matter the color of your hair. You know how they are: slaves to their animal natures," Elena confided.

"But don't you have an animal nature, Elena?' Gwyneth asked.

"I did once, dear, but it got me into real trouble," Elena said, and she put down her yarn. Her mind reverted back to the days of her marriage.

"Gwyneth, honey, my daddy is a Missionary Baptist preacher, and he is all about teaching people to live without some parts of them-selves," Elena said after ten minutes of silence.

"I wasn't raised in the church," Gwyneth said in a loud voice, "so I

79.

am not gonna listen to talk like that," the girl said.

The music that night on WDXR Radio 6 was good. There was a reason why it was the most popular radio station in Greenville.

"Well, I haven't trapped a man yet, but I have them all staring at me," Gwyneth said and she sat up.

She twisted her body around to the front of the couch and stood. She walked over to the window which was dirty with grime.

"I gotta do something with myself, Elena," she said with a faint sob in her voice. "I am goin crazy, honey," she managed to say.

The young woman then walked briskly to the kitchenette and got down on her knees. She opened a cabinet door under the sink and took out a blue plastic bucket and a half empty bottle of Mr. Clean. She grabbed a plastic brush from inside the cabinet, put the bucket under the faucet of the sink and filled it half-full of water. She poured the bottle of Mr. Clean into the bucket of water and got down on all fours and started furiously scrubbing the linoleum floor with the sudsy water.

At nine o'clock that night, Elena put down her yarn and trudged to the back bed room. In Elena and Gwyneth's apartment, the front room with Elena's chair and Gwyneth's couch was kept relatively tidy. The kitchenette in the rear of the room and the bedroom in the back were always in disarray. The blanket's on Elena's bed were bunched into a ball on top of the mattress. The cover slips on her pillows were half off the pillows revealing the faded yellow material beneath. The two feather pillows at the head of the bed had been bought used, and so the feathers had gathered to one side of the pillows leaving the opposite side flat and uncomfortable. To com-pensate, Elena folded the pillows over on themselves to make them bulkier.

"Next week, I am gonna wash everything in here," she said upon entering the bedroom.

She straightened the wrinkled flat sheet and grabbed both corners of the blanket. With a sharp upward movement of her arms, she lifted the blanket into the air and watched it fall slowly down upon the mattress. Elena undressed, putting her bedclothes on a wooden chair in the corner of the room. She pulled a floral night gown about her still lithe and youthful body. Then she lay down upon the bed and mused to the sound of Gwyneth scrubbing the floor of the kitchenette.

"Maybe I should be more like Gwyneth and Beth," she thought. "I am very pretty and very nice," she thought sadly. Somewhere in Greenville there has to be a decent man who only wants to make a woman like me happy," she reflected. "I don't know why life has to be so hard. Life here in Greenville is just not fair," she thought and then she drifted off to sleep.

Elena's apartment was only a half mile from Sanchez Grocery. It was often her habit to walk to work and back home again each day. It was Spring and she was walking to work early one morning. The air was brisk and there was a feeling of dampness from a recent rainfall. Elena had appropriate clothes for walking in all seasons of the year. In the Spring and Autumn, when rain was frequent, she wore a long coat that her parents had given her ten years before on her birthday. As she entered the grocery, Rosa, now in her fifties, was sweeping in front of the cash register.

"Elena...Tall man ask for you last night after you go home," Rosa mentioned.

"Rosa, I do not have any close men friends. What did he look like?" Elena asked.

"Not bad looking, honey. He have pretty smile," her boss told her.

"I hope you did not tell him anything about me. You have me worried," Elena said in an excited voice.

81.

"I tell him nothing," Rosa said flatly. "If he like you, he be back," she said.

Although Elena was a quiet person, her mind worked at a furious pace. After Rosa's news about the gentleman admirer, Elena began paying strict attention to the male clientele of the grocery. There were not many men who shopped there. The younger women often brought children with them. The older women, like Wayne's Shelley, shopped alone. Two weeks after Rosa's news, Elena had completed her review of the store's male clientele. The majority of the male prospects were like the hapless detective at the Market Street Diner who tried to talk to Elena.

Kenneth was a frequent shopper at Sanchez Grocery. He had been noticing the pretty woman with off-color blue hair for years. Kenneth was fifty-five years old. His wife had been killed in a car wreck eight years before the present time. Since the death of his wife friends has tried to fix him up with available bachelorettes. However, for some reason, he had never hit it off with any of them. It was Saturday evening and Kenneth was alone in his small house on the outskirts of Greenville. His job in middle-management at a local lumber warehouse paid only a modest salary. Not one to complain about money, he had stayed at the warehouse while many of his single men friends had job-hopped looking for large paychecks. Kenneth loved to cook and tonight he was frying skin-less chicken for soft-shell, Mexican tacos. The flat bread for the tacos was from Sanchez Grocery.

"I think I like both types of tortillas," he told himself.

He had tried both the corn meal and wheat flour tortillas. The salsa that he used was of the "extra-hot" variety. After frying the meat, he made three tacos and grabbed a bottle of salsa. Then he sat down at the round table in his kitchen. For a beverage he had his usual southern, sweet tea with ice.

"She does not look up at me when I shop at the Mexican grocery,"

82.

He thought glumly. "She probably already has a boyfriend. That would just be my luck," he said to himself.

"I don't know why I have waited so long to try to get to know her?" He thought. "I must be a real idiot," he mumbled while munching one of the tacos.

"Pretty boy...You do nuthin," Kenneth heard someone beside him say. It was a Thursday evening at Sanchez Grocery. It had been two months since he had stopped Rosa and asked her about her clerk. He put a can of refried beans into his shopping basket and turned his head only to see Rosa staring him squarely in the face.

"You got pretty boy smile...but you say nuthin to our Elena," the short Mexican woman complained.

"Oh, Elena...is that her name?" He asked.

Kenneth's mood brightened as he spoke to Rosa. "Elena is such a pretty name for such a nice woman," he said.

Rosa came close to Kenneth and looked up at him. "She tell me say nuthin to you," and then Rosa chuckled. "I say nuthin, she live her whole life alone," and Rosa felt a tear forming in her eye.

"That girl, honey, she better than any man deserve," Rosa said and then started to walk away.

Kenneth called after Rosa, "I want to be a good friend to your pretty clerk," he said.

Rosa halted and turned back, "I know honey. You been here long time, never cause trouble," she said.

With Rosa's exit, Kenneth walked to the back aisle where he knew Elena was working stocking the shelves. He approached her and stood beside her as she put packages of dried noodles on the shelf. He turned his head and looked at her, and then froze, unable to speak.

"Elena looked up, "if you are looking for noodles, sir, try these," she said and then she handed him one of the packages.

"Thank you," he said looking down into her pale blue eyes. Then he walked nervously back to the front of the grocery.

85.

A Brief Sketch

"Life can be cruel," Joseph reflected.

On the radio that day, he had heard that a ten year old Guatemalan boy had died in US custody on the Mexican-US border. Migrant caravans were camped out, escaping from the drug wars in Central America. The US president had frozen government worker's pay and then shut down the Federal Government over a border wall dispute concerning illegal immigrants from Central America. Workers were struggling to make ends meet often without success. Joseph sat by himself in a largely empty Hardees. It was early in the morning and a variety of day laborers came and went ordering breakfast on their way to work. It had been a cold March day. He took out a cigarette, put on his Miami Marlins coat and stepped outside. He lit up a cigarette and took a draw. Watching the cars go by the CVS drugstore, he wondered how long he had to live.

Joseph was seventy-two years old. His wife had died ten years earlier. She had been on dialysis for years and at age fifty-nine she told her physician that she could not face another session of dialysis. The nephrologist informed the couple that she would not last another ten days without medical treatment. Joseph and his wife, resigned to the inevitable, waited. After a week, Josephs' wife lost consciousness. The end was not easy to watch. His father had died at age seventy-five from lung cancer. His father had been, like Joseph, a smoker, but had never before been sick a day in his life. But now, his father was coughing blood and after one week was having difficulty walking. The family took him to the local emergency room where he was quickly admitted to the hospital. When Joseph and his family arrived at the nursing station on his father's floor, the old man was already dead.

"That gives me about three more years," Joseph thought to himself.

He pulled his Miami Marlins jacket around his thin frame and watched as the smoke from his cigarette rose in the cold, Spring air.

A week later he was in the local primary care doctor's office. He was called back and weighed: one hundred and forty pounds. Jenny, the nurse, escorted him to the examination room and once he was seated, she took his blood pressure and pulse. Joseph looked at Jenny. She was about thirty-five years old, brunette, and about fifteen pounds too heavy.

"I guess the stress is gettin to her," he thought.

Jenny had two boys-ages eight and twelve. Her husband was an Emergency Medical Technologist at the local ambulance agency. Joseph had been getting short of breath. He had finally come to the point where more trips to the chiropractor would be useless. He then made his appointment with Doc. Brown. After Doc. Brown listened to Joseph's complaints, he took out his stethoscope and examined Joseph's heart and lungs. He then noticed the clubbing of Joseph's fingernails and sent him to X-Ray for a chest X-ray. Joseph was told that the diagnosis was emphysema.

"It's those cigarettes you are smoking," the doctor said rudely.

"What the hell do you know? You are a quack anyway!" Joseph had said loudly and then walked out.

"He's only in it for the money," Joseph told himself as he drove off in his red Toyota truck.

He felt unnerved by his argument with Doc. Brown, so he drove to the city mountain park for solitude and to do a little hiking. He sat alone in his truck at the park. After about thirty-minutes, he got out and hiked up to Huckleberry Ridge. Every fifty feet or so, he had to stop to catch his breath. His heart rate increased along with the gasps of breath. He managed to make the ridge and then he sat down on a bench in a graveled clearing. The valley below was a pretty site. It was early March and only the understory of the forest floor had leafed out. A few small, white flowers were blooming. Joseph could hear the lonely call of a pilieated wood pecker in the distance. As his breathing slowed, he began to relax. His legs had the pleasant feeling of physical exertion. He stood up and made his way back down to his parked truck.

During the day, Joseph wandered about the city. He had a rented room in an old Federal style farmhouse. His landlady, Ruth, was a widow. She had a daughter and granddaughter. Joseph lived upstairs in one of three bedrooms. Downstairs, he had a bathroom and kitchen privileges. The kitchen was a large, country-style kitch-en with a gas stove and a wood-burning fireplace in one corner. In the mornings, Joseph and Ruth ate breakfast together. Ruth was a good cook, and she had taught her tenant how to make homemade biscuits and corn bread. Through the window over the sink, Joseph could see the chickens running about the backyard. He loved the old elm tree behind the house.

About six p.m. Joseph entered the front hall of the farmhouse and walked back to the kitchen. He sat down at the table in a steel chair with a green, plastic cushion seat.

"What's cookin?" he asked as Ruth bustled about the room.

"What're you havin?" was the reply.

"There was a sale at Food City, and I bought some Polish sausage and sauerkraut. It's good for what ails ya," Joseph replied.

Ruth answered, "I'll have it all out and ready in an hour," she said.

Soon, a large aluminum pot was boiling on the stove with the ingre-dients for the night's meal.

"How are things at Hardees?" Ruth asked Joseph.

"April was in a fix. Only three employees showed up this morning. Bob transferred back from Hardees in Erwin. It's good to see him back. He won two wrestling matches at his gym. He's the club champion now," Joseph related.

"It'd be good if sum of his matches turned into money," Ruth replied.

After dinner Joseph helped Ruth wash the dishes and then he went up to his room. He sat down in a large rocking chair and turned on the radio. The news was not very encouraging. The government shut down was in its third week. Some of the out-of-work government employees had defaulted on their mortgage payments and the banks who held the loans were pressuring them. The older Federal employees had stopped buying their prescription drugs. Food was a priority and so far, those who were struggling were not going without food. The President had bragged that he was willing to let the shutdown last many months. Morale among the government employees was at a record low. Joseph knew some of the Mexican immigrant workers in the area. He knew they were not terrorists.

"On the other hand, if they are illegal, they will have to go," he thought.

Turning off the radio, he reached for his guitar. A friend who had passed away had left it to him, otherwise, he could not have afforded the custom-built instrument. He began strumming and finger-picking one of his favorite Bluegrass tunes.

It was seven-thirty a.m. and Joseph sat at his place in Hardees. The usual people were there: a group of well-to-do businessmen on the other side of the room discussed their golf games. In the corner, next to the businessmen sat a podiatrist and his wife. They usually came in formal clothes and looked out-of-place. The podiatrist had his hair curled. His wife wore an expensive dress. This generated some resentment from the usual patrons of Hardees who were working class. Raoul and his friends from a lawn care business were there, and there was Bob who worked the front counter. Bob seemed oblivious to the businessmen and the podiatrist couple. Each morning Bob circulated around the dining room filling cups of coffee. On his shirt he wore a button which read "donate." The migrant workers never failed to put their excess change in a jar on the front counter for the needy.

"Hey buddy, thanks for the pay day loan last week," Bob said to Joseph as he filled Joseph's coffee cup. "I am fighting at the West Market Fight Club this weekend. Why don't you drop in and watch?" Bob asked Joseph.

"Okay," Joseph said.

Joseph privately wondered why Bob considered being slammed to the floor fun. Bob was tall and broad and he had the large belly of an amateur wrestler. He had taken and given many beatings and seemed to thrive on it. Although Bob was an amateur, he had a friend who acted as his promoter. When Bob fought his matches, he wore a thick black belt with a large silver buckle.

Saturday night at ten p.m. Joseph entered the West Market Fight Club and sat at a ringside table. The early match was winding down. Bob and his opponent, the Unicoi Wasp, were preparing for their match. They entered the ring from their corners and began flailing away at each other. Joseph winced, looked away and then stared down at his diet coke. Joseph had been sober since his late thirties.

Amid the groans and thumps of bodies being slammed against the mat came a voice through the smoky air, "poppy buy me a drink?"

Joseph looked up and his eyes met a young-looking female face framed in blonde curls. She was dressed in low-cut jeans and a tank top.

"Okay, darlin, take a seat," he responded. "The night is lookin up," he thought. "I'll take a vodka on the rocks," she said.

90.

Sally slurped down her vodka on the rocks, and asked for another. She chatted about her life off the farm and how much she enjoyed living in Greenville. Joseph wondered if she had a steady boyfriend and who her parents were. He knew better than to ask these questions.

After about two hours and fifty dollars, he reached over and took her drink," that's enough honey," he said.

Abruptly, Sally stood up from her chair and walked away. In a distant part of the room, Joseph heard her hustling another old man.

The red Toyota truck chugged down the road in Unicoi County. The road was narrow and the land was hilly. Most of the region had been logged off over one-hundred years ago. The cleared land was rocky. A few twisted trees could be seen amid herds of goats and cattle. Joseph pulled into a driveway in front of a small, brick house. A young woman with brunette hair answered the door after a few knocks.

"Does Bob want company?" Joseph asked Abby.

"Of course, come in and sit a spell," Abby answered.

The living room was dark. Bob was seated in a chair in the back of the room with his arm in a cast.

"Man, you took a whuppin Saturday night," Joseph said to his friend.

Bob rapped the cast with the knuckles of his left hand. "Hard to get me down," he replied. "Next time, I will be the one to do the damage," Bob said.

"He's tough and ken take whatever the other guy can dish out," Abby bragged. "Have sum apple pie?" Abby asked as she cut a

91.

piece from the dish on the table.

"Please," Joseph said.

It was an unusually cold morning for April. There were few cars on
the road early Sunday morning. The red truck pulled into a parking
space at Hardees. Joseph sat in his truck listening to the radio.
A local man had been gunned down at the county dump the day
before. There were roadblocks coming into Greenville all looking
for a white, over-sized truck fitting a certain description. As Joseph
climbed out of the cab, he began a hacking cough. The coughing
became uncontrollable, and his chest heaved with the effort. There
were streaks of blood in the phlegm that he spat out onto the concrete of the Hardees parking lot. While he was walking toward the
door of the restaurant, a small, rusted car with North Carolina plates
pulled up beside him.

"I'm on my way back to North Carolina, and I need money to feed
my boy," a woman said.

There was a plump toddler on the seat beside the woman. Joseph
took out his wallet and pulled out all the money he had inside.

He leaned over and gave the money to her.

"Happy Easter," he said to her.

93.

A Student's Life

Michael shared three rooms with his brother. The two of them
came and went and seldom met. His brother had dropped out of
school two years before. Michael had never been to his brother's
place of work, but he knew his brother's job had something to do
with the police. Frank had a number of friends who were detec-
tives and patrol officers. One Wednesday night, Michael met his
brother and a police-woman at an all-night grill. The conversation
was grisly, but his brother and the police-woman were cheerful and
upbeat. Mable was a blonde in her forties. She was short, with
closely cropped hair and a loud laugh. The grill cooks were in a
good mood on this particular night. The heat of the cook surface
and the steam that rose from it contrasted with the dark chill of the
night outside.

"I had those two dead to rights," Mable chuckled.

"Were they carrying during the collar?" Frank asked.

"Hell, yeah, they were carrying, but I had the heat out of their pockets lickity split," she continued. "They are sittin in jail as we speak,"
she said, and the two friends laughed.

Michael sat nearby concentrating on a plate of scrambled eggs.

Back in his apartment, Michael reviewed the events of the day:
three lectures-one at ten, one at twelve, and one at three o'clock.
During his freshman year at college, he had an eight a.m. class-for
the first and last time.

"A paper to complete; that can be put off for another two weeks,"
he thought. "Midterms are coming up. I better begin typing my
hand-written notes," he said to himself.

By ten o'clock that night, several composition books of notes had
been typed and he put the typewriter away. His picked up his bar-

bells and began working out. After fifty catch-and-release moves, his back began to hurt so he lay the weights on the floor and climbed into bed.

The next day was Saturday. Michael slept late. In the early after-noon, about two p.m., he roused himself from sleep and looked around his bed. His shirt and jeans had been thrown on the top of a chest of drawers. His shoes took some effort to locate. Once he was dressed, he went out. On the street, he headed north. The apartment that Michael shared with Frank was in downtown Lex-ington. It was two flights above Goldberg's Pawn Shop. Bill and Jennifer lived one floor below them. As he walked the street he saw Trixie, a fellow college student, hawking magazines. He had seen Trixie in Anthropology class.

"I'll take "Science Fantasy Today," Michael smiled at Trixie and held out his money.

Trixie fumbled with her stack of magazines, searching for "Science Fantasy Today." "Hey, you look familiar," she exclaimed.

"Anthropology class," he replied.

Trixie looked puzzled. There were probably close to one-hundred students in Anthropology class at the university. In Michael's opin-ion, however, Trixie had stood out among the other coeds in class. She was naturally a brunette, but she had dyed streaks of purple into her hair. Despite the odd coloring, her hair was becoming and she had it pulled back into a pony-tail. During the week, rather than selling magazines, she waited tables at a noodle shop on Main Street. Michael had become an unnoticed regular customer there.

Putting the magazine in his back pocket, Michael turned right at the next corner onto Main Street. He surveyed the shops along the street. Many of the shops were closed this afternoon. Two adult book stores were open. The bars and discotheques of downtown would open at six p.m. The city did not keep downtown in good shape. The surroundings were shabby. There were potholes in the asphalt. The pavement of the sidewalks was uneven. Whole slabs of concrete were slightly tilted at odd angles and there were noticeable gaps between the slabs. Litter on the street and along the sidewalks was common. Michael was familiar with the occasional brown empty beer bottles laying near the fronts of the downtown businesses.

He stopped at a gun-barrel style diner and went inside and sat at a stool behind the counter that ran along the front window. He ordered lunch and opened the magazine to read. His mind, however was on Trixie.

Trixie was a vision that Michael had never known. She was young and cute. She had a teenage freshness about her, and her manner was perky. He felt happy just thinking about her, despite the fact that he had barely spoken to her. He wondered what her life was like.

"What were her plans for the future and where would her life lead? Did she have someone?" he wondered.

In high school, three years before, he had been desperately lonely. A good student, he was considered odd by the popular crowd. While the pretty girls in school had been chauffeured from date to date by boys with well-to-do fathers, Michael had spent all of his time working at a grocery store to save money for college. Needless to say, he didn't date. At his Senior Prom, he and the other blue-collar boys had gone dateless and stood in the corner of the ballroom while his better off classmates had danced. Frankly, he thought, "I am glad to put all of that behind me."

Back in his apartment, the cursing and screaming from Bill and Jennifer one floor below increased in volume. Jennifer let Bill feel the full weight of her displeasure. As Bill's wife, she expected to be kept up and cared for. Bill, a co-owner of several downtown bars wanted Jenniferr to help in the bars.

96.
 After thirty minutes of screaming, a door could be heard opening
and then there was the rumble of feet descending the stairs. Then
the exterior door to the apartments slammed shut.

The phone rang and Michael picked up: it was Frank. "Oh, that's
just Jennifer and Bill. It's not going to get any better," Frank explained to Michael.

Later, Frank came home and the two brothers shared a pizza.
There was an eerie silence from Bill and Jennifer's apartment. Just
before midnight, pounding began from the exterior door downstairs.
Bill was locked out, and as far as Jennifer was concerned, he
wasn't getting back in. The two brothers wondered if life had to be
this hard.

Marriage, at that time, appeared to be a precarious state of exis-
tence to Michael. Most of his married buddies were not happy with
their wives. Yes, his friends were in school and the women were
supporting them. But they were also supposed to have wives; not
just live-in roommates. There was the ironing, the cleaning, the
preparing of food, and the paying of bills. Really, should a full-time
student be expected to do housework? And then there were the
hen parties. The wives just were not around much of the time. In
search of excitement, the husbands caroused the strip bars and
drank. Infidelity was routine, and so were the crude arguments-the
stress of husband and wife living together. Many marriages lasted
five years or less.

"It makes sense to wait, or just not go there," he told himself. "Single life is preferable," he thought.

 Weeks later, found Trixie working late that night. The clientele of
the shop had been boorish. One large man put a hand where it
was not welcome. A quick slap across his face resulted. Most of

97.
the men who frequented the shop were single and hard up. Tips
were low. As the evening wore on, Trixie's hair became mussed by
all the running around carrying plates of food to the tables. Later
that night a slim young man quietly look his seat and ordered. He
seemed polite; she was surprised. Trixie noticed him look away
after making eye contact with her. He didn't say much and spoke
with a soft voice. She felt relaxed around him. He was not like the
hardened customers she constantly dealt with. After the young
man left, she felt let down. His large tip left for her came as a sur-
prise.

Michael had been dining at the noodle shop for quite some time,
but still Trixie had not noticed him. He had tried to get her attention,
not knowing how to introduce himself. How could he come across
as different, not just another male looking for excitement? He felt
she was just as unhappy as he was. Like all young adults, she was
overworked and underpaid.

"What can I offer a girl like her?" He asked himself. He was perpetually broke. "She needs an older man, out of school, who can bring
home an income," he reflected.

After he left the large tip for Trixie at the Asian noodle shop, he
walked home to his apartment. Climbing the two flights of stairs, he
noticed that all was quiet with Jennifer and Bill. As he closed the
door upon entering his apartment, he could feel the cold linoleum
through the soles of his shoes. He sat down in a chair and pulled
the shoes off...holes in both soles. He grabbed a pair of scissors
and cut two pieces of cardboard from a box. He stuffed the cardboard into the shoes.

It was a long walk to class every day, several miles from downtown
to the main campus. Michael's car had been parked in a pay-for
city lot for six months. The battery in the car was dead. It made
sense for him to walk. He could have ridden his bike, but it had
been stolen the semester before. One day, on campus, he was on

98.

his way to Biology class. He was looking off into the distance, and
he decided to look into the faces of the students. No one looked
back; they all stared off into the distance as if he didn't exist. The
long train of humanity on campus: the menagerie of faces was
interesting.

"What are their stories? Where will they end up?" He asked himself.

Lunch at the cafeteria had at one time been a struggle just to get
through the lines. To compensate, Michael showed up one hour
early before the mass of people. Breakfast was out of the question.
Eight o'clock was much too early to be up. It was better to sleep an
extra couple of hours. In class, before lunch, he had trouble with
his stomach making noises. Well, that was the price he paid for the
comfort of staying in bed late and skipping breakfast. Some of the
other students had boycotted the cafeteria claiming that the food
was bad. To Michael, the food was good, even though the servings
were too small.

On the weekends downtown, the lights of the city were on. It was
late at night one weekend, and Michael felt depressed. He found
twenty dollars in the drawer and headed out north on the sidewalk
of downtown. Along Upper Street he stopped at O'Keefe's Jazz
Club. He climbed the single flight of stairs to the club. Once inside,
he paid the cover charge and sat in the back. He felt lucky to get a
seat that night. A band from Detroit was giving the customers a feel
for the music of Aretha's hometown. Stobe lights gave the stage an
electric look. The horns and guitars were loud. Drinks were expensive, so he sipped his drink slowly. After an hour he felt better. A
night like this at O'Keefe's would last him weeks. He left and made
his way back home.

The next semester Michael awoke early and turned the radio on.
It was a cold February. A major snowstorm had hit Lexington that
night. The university and its cafeterias were closed for the day.
This was a welcome change from the routine of class. He could
look forward to a day in his apartment. His brother, Frank, was

99.

asleep in the corner, having come home early in the morning. The city's snow plows had been out during the night clearing the streets. Main Street was in good shape, but several feet of snow had collected near the sidewalks. The merchants of downtown had been clearing a path for their customers through the frozen precipitation. About noon, Michael headed for the noodle shop.

The bell on the door of the Asian shop tinkled as he entered and then sat down. Trixie was in the rear with her back to him taking an order. He noticed her familiar blue and purple hair. After a long wait, she approached his table with her pad and pencil in hand.

"Can I take your order?" She asked.

Michael looked up and said, "hi."

"Uh, okay...Hi...What would you like?" She asked again.

Trixie fumbled nervously with her order pad.

"I'll have the usual vegetable low mein. I've seen you here quite a bit," he said.

'Yes, well I do put in a lot of hours," Trixie's body stiffened and she felt the warmth rising in her cheeks.

It had been a long time since a man had struck up a conversation with her. She felt the excitement of having attracted male attention. She smiled encouragingly and left to put in the order with the cook. A boy brought Michael's low mein, but he expected Trixie to collect the money from the check. He was not disappointed. When his plate was empty Trixie made her appearance and placed the bill on the table. No bank in Lexington would give Michael a credit card so he always paid in cash.

As Trixie counted out the change, he looked up at her and said, "I'm Michael."

100.

The young woman could not restrain a smile from spreading across her face. She didn't say anything but quickly retreated to the back of the restaurant. Michael put his usual, large tip under the plate and exited the restaurant.

After the door of the shop closed behind him, Trixie hurried to the front window and watched his figure as it receded down the snowy sidewalk. She was excited and worried.

Finally, she lost sight of Michael. She then glanced around the tired-looking eatery and whispered, "he will be back."

101.

Carl in Three Parts

102.

Part One

A blue and white station wagon pulled onto the dusty, graveled parking lot of the farm supply store. A man got out from the driver's side. In addition to this solitary human occupant, the station wagon contained three dogs. The side view and rear view windows of the car were covered in dirt. The front windshield was dirty as well, but the activity of two worn windshield wipers had created arc-like regions of clear glass on either side of the station wagon's windshield.

The driver of the car, like his vehicle, looked worn. The clerk of the farm supply watched him with interest as he walked through the parking lot to the concrete porch of the store, climbed its four steps and ambled inside.

"You from around here, neighbor?" The clerk asked Carl.

"Montana, I am from Montana," Carl said.

"What ken I do for you today, then?" The clerk asked. "I am lookin for a place for me and my animals," Carl said.

"How much ken you pay then?" Carl was asked.

"I ain't lookin for nuthin fancy, young man, and I ain't lookin to buy," the old man said.

"Well then, go down to the Budget 6 on Highway 45 bout three miles south and you will find yer place," he was told.

Carl was sixty-eight years old, twice divorced, and ten years alone at this time. Alone, that is except for Buddy, Bingo, and Blaze-the animal passengers in his blue and white station wagon. To anyone willing to look him over he wasn't worth much, either as a friend or as a customer. He bought fifty pounds of dried dog food and re-treated down the steps of the farm supply toward his vehicle.

103.

In the area in which Carl had just arrived, strangers like him were shunned. This was the way of this small, western Kentucky town. Well, you could say he had arrived in a town, or more correctly, you could say he had arrived at a four-way stop with a drive-in restaurant and a farm supply. Other than these two businesses and the Budget 6 motel south of the four-way, the land was dotted with small farms. On the weekends all the farmers of the area gathered at the hog auctions. In the Spring they were at the Big Burley tobacco market. Otherwise, not much went on in the county.

The blue and white station wagon soon pulled onto the blacktop of the Budget 6. Carl had some trouble getting out of the car and onto his feet. His short legs were bowed slightly and he walked with a prominent limp. The limp was the result of a high-school football injury back in Bozeman. Walking took some effort and Carl walked at a slow pace. It was hot today. The month was July. The air-conditioning in the Budget 6 had been broken for weeks. Billy, the manager of the Budget 6, had elected not to spend the cash for repairs so far this summer. To cool the office room, the aluminum and glass door to the small office stood propped open by a red brick. The strong smell of ten days of cross-country driving followed Carl into the office. Billy frowned at the smell and he became suspicious of the man as he approached the desk.

"How much a month is the rent here?" Carl asked looking up at Billy, who was tall and thin.

"Three hundred," Billy said tersely.

"I'll take six months to start, and I will write you a check up front," Carl offered.

"Don't think so, stranger," Billy said. "I don't know you any more than them dogs you got ridin in yer car," he said.

'You just call my bank and ask them about me. My name is Carl Trep," the man said.

"Okay, but I don't think it will do the likes of you any good," was the reply.

Carl took a short pencil from his front trouser pocket and put the tip of the pencil in his mouth to moisten it. He scribbled an out-of-town number on the front of a piece of newspaper and handed the paper to Billy.

"Just call. It will be worth your while," Carl said and he walked back to sit in his car.

"Bank of Bozeman, good morning," Billy heard upon calling the number. "Gotta man here, name of Carl Trep. Wants to write a check for bout two thousand dollars," Billy said into the phone.

"Yes, okay, accept his check for any amount he writes," the bank employee said.

"Yer, kiddin," Billy exclaimed. "You think I am sum kinda fool?" He asked loudly into the phone.

"If you don't take Mr. Trep's check, then you are a fool," the voice from Montana said. "You can take a check for any amount he wants to write as I told you," the bank repeated.

Billy hung up the phone and walked outside to the driver's side of the station wagon. "You gotta room, mister," he said. "Come on inside and write yer check. Don't mind me. I don't git in no one's way, even sum stranger frum a place like Bozeman," he said to Carl. As Billy spoke to Carl, he counted three dogs inside the back of the car. "Them dogs is welcome, just like you," Billy said and he walked back inside the office of the Budget 6.

Later that afternoon, Ethel watched through the front window of her room as an older stranger and three dogs moved into the room next to her. Ethel had lived at the Budget 6 for five years. She was older than Billy, who was about fifty years old at the time. Billy was her deceased sister's only son. Living at the Budget 6 was good for both Billy and Ethel. Billy had trouble finding help around the motel.

105.

When money was tight for Ethel, she could work off her rent. After watching her neighbor for about fifteen minutes, Ethel stood up
from the green sofa that stood against the front window of her room
and walked back to the bathroom.

Ethel had been working on her appearance. She had dyed her
gray hair an orange brown.

"The color is okay," she thought, having gone through the aisle of
hair products at the drug store in Mayfield.

As was the custom of the women of her era, Ethel visited the beauty parlor every week. "What else do I have to spend money on?"
She asked herself. "The only places to eat out around here are the
hamburger joints and the fried chicken places," she acknowledged
to herself.

Each week her thin, orange hair was wound into tight curls all over
her head and then sprayed down with a heavy hair spray to control
the loose ends.

"I hate to tell Ethel, but her hair looks like it is made of plastic," Billy
thought silently one day.

Ethel was older, but she had not totally "gone to seed" where her
appearance was concerned. Her girlfriends had few enjoyments in
life other than cooking and eating. They had lost their girlish figures
years ago and had now gained considerable weight.

"It don't matter how fat I am," Ethel's friend Mabel said to her one
day, "cause I wear pretty fashions."

Ethel wisely kept her tongue and agreed with Mabel.

In many ways, Ethel was a remarkable woman. She had refrained
from overeating and had remained thin. But to her dismay, no matter how many inches she lost around her waist, her stomach still
protruded beyond the contour of her flat chest.

"When I was a young gal," she reflected, "the ol stomach here was as flat as a board and my bosom was rounded and firm."

She knew this to be a fact because, until she was about fifty years old, Ethel had been a heart-breaker among the local bachelors.

The next week, on Wednesday afternoon, Billy was manning the front desk at the motel. Carl walked in. He had two dogs on leashes that followed obediently behind him. Billy could see that they were not expensive dogs, despite the fact that he knew Carl was rich.

"Mutt dogs is just right for a beat-up ol man like him," Billy thought as he looked up from the desk. Billy surveyed the occupants of his front office from behind the desk.

There was dirty Carl, with his paunchy stomach and bowed legs. His blue shirt was open at the top displaying a chest of gray hair and coffee stains.

"I guess he don't care where the coffee ends up when he is drinkin," Billy thought. "Why don't that man wash his front if he spills coffee down his shirt?" he asked himself.

Standing beside Carl were two of this three canine companions.

"Whur's yer third mutt, friend?" Billy asked him.

 "Bingo is in solitary confinement at present," Carl answered. "He doesn't get along with these two," Carl continued.

Billy looked at the two animals on leashes, "whut names do you call them two?" he asked.

"Well, the little one here is Buddy and the big one there is Blaze," Carl said in reply.

107.

To Billy, Buddy and Blaze were opposites of the canine spectrum:
Buddy was a very small mongrel with short black hair on top and
skinny brown and white legs below. Buddy panted eagerly, looking
up at the tall fifty-ish human. Blaze, on the other hand, looked ex-
ceedingly strange. He had the large head of a Siberian husky and
the long shaggy coat of a collie. By all appearances, Blaze had not
been trimmed in a very long time. His long fur coat, colored brown
and black was of uneven and ungainly lengths.

"This big one is bout as ugly as a dog ken get," Billy realized.

Suddenly, Buddy began barking furiously and lunging toward the
desk behind which stood the manager.

"I bet that little guy ken bite like hell," Billy said loudly.

"Nope, he has never bitten anyone and never will," Carl said.

Billy took a piece of bacon from a plate on the counter and walked
around to Buddy.

"Here doggy, try this," he said as he held out the bacon.

Buddy grabbed it eagerly with his teeth, not bothering to spare the
human's finger tips from the clamp of his jaws.

"I hope you are a'feedin him enough. He seems mighty eager to
snap at me," Billy replied.

"Buddy just needs time to calm down in this strange place. He is
used to running the fields back home," the bow-legged man said.

Then Carl jerked the two leashes vigorously and pulled the two
dogs out of the office and the three walked back to their motel
room.

A slow wail, like the distant howl of a wolf began later that night.

Ethel slept fitfully and her mind struggled with the uncomfortable sound of the howl. Then, the dark room around her was still and silent. Ethel had thought for years that she just did not have dreams.

I don't know if I don't dream or I am just too old the remember anythin anymore," she sometimes wondered.

When she was young she had vivid romantic dreams of her and the many boyfriends who had courted her. Living life was something she once did, now she just existed. A sharp, high-pitched yapping sound intruded into her consciousness. She woke suddenly to a loud barking and scraping sound on the wall of the adjoining room.

"I am gonna murder my damn neighbor and his confounded animals," she cursed as she sat up in bed.

A ruckus was going on in the next room.

"Don't them dogs get sleepy?" Ethel wondered.

The rent at the Budget 6 was cheap and the walls were thin. There was very little privacy. She stood up and walked over to the wall between Carl's room and her room, and began pounding it with her fists. Soon the phone rang. It was Billy.

"Honey, try to quiet down; the ol man cain't sleep," Billy said over the phone.

"Whut's he doin complaining to you at night fer?" She nearly shouted. "The whole business in his room has been drivin me crazy for nearly an hour," she answered, not caring how she sounded.

Ethel then hung up on her nephew and returned to bed. Fortunately for both Billy and Ethel, their phone conversation coincided with an end to the turmoil in Carl's room. Ethel resolved the next day to talk to her nephew about the problem.

Five days after Ethel and Billy had talked about the new occupants of the Budget 6, Billy sat behind the counter in the front office. From this vantage point he could see all the coming and going of the renters of the motel. He had been putting off talking to Carl about his dogs.

"I don't know this guy from Montana much," he reflected.

Billy didn't like conflict with renters, but at the Budget 6 conflict was part of the job. The springs of his metal chair squeaked as he stood up. Carl and one of the dogs had just gone into their room next door to Ethel.

"Yep," Carl answered in a gruff voice as he opened the door to Billy.

"Hey, neighbor, let's me and you talk sum," Billy said nervously.

"Bout whut, mister boss man?" Carl answered looking directly into Billy's eyes.

"Jus let me in. I don't mean no harm," Billy pleaded.

"Well, come on inside and sit down," Carl responded quickly. "Do you like chili?" Carl asked as the two men walked inside.

The room was dark despite the fact that the time was mid-day. All of the blinds were drawn shut. As Billy walked inside and sat at a table he saw a large, fierce-looking Chow dog eyeing him from the corner.

"Who's that guy over there, friend?" He asked Carl as the two sat at a round table near the wall.

"That's Bingo. I tol you bout him. He spends most of his time in solitary," Carl answered briefly.

"Billy laughed nervously, "I reckon this here big doggy don't get along with anyone," Billy said.

"Yes and no," Carl replied. "He got in a fight in Bozeman, just before we headed East, and he got one a his legs bloodied up," Carl explained.

"It's too damn noisy at night in here mister," Billy said suddenly under his breath.

"I figured that might be a problem with my nice lady neighbor," Carl acknowledged. "Whut we gonna do bout it?" Billy asked.

"Me and my dogs don't want to be a problem," Carl said earnestly. "But sometimes things get rowdy," he explained. "I ken put a muzzle on anyone who gets excited."

"That'll help neighbor. The ol woman next door ken make a lot of noise on her own," the landlord explained. "Whut's that smell, friend?" Billy asked sniffing the air.

"It's chili, want sum?" Carl asked.

"Okay, I really like Mexican food," he replied to Carl. Soon Carl sat down with two bowls of chili and two cans of beer between them.

The two men began eating silently. Then, after a few minutes, Carl got up and went into the back of room. Returning, he brought his check book.

"Look, boss man," he said. "Bingo over there in the corner and Buddy and Blaze in the back of the room are all I got in the world," he explained.

He then became silent and began writing in the check book. "If you think it'll help, I'll pay double rent," he said as he held out the thin paper.

Ethel and Mabel sat at Mabel's kitchen table on a Sunday afternoon. The time of the year was Summer and Mabel's husband and her two grown sons had finished bringing in the garden. It didn't matter to Mabel that there were no good restaurants in the region, because she could cook just about anything that was pleasing to the palate. In the other room sat Tommy, Mabel's husband and three of his hunting companions all watching sports on the television.

"I tol Buehla last Friday that if she doesn't get my color right, I am changing shops," Mabel said to Ethel as she pushed a large piece of applesauce cake into her plump mouth.

"Don't tell me Tommy is complainin about the way you look, honey?" Ethel said.

"He dont complain. That ain't the problem," Mabel said. "The problem is he has dun forgot how to talk," she said.

"He don't need to talk, honey, cause he can use up all his time listnin to you," Ethel said with a grin.

"Have things quieted down with the old man next door?" Mabel asked her friend. Ethel thought as she cut a piece of Dutch apple pie.

"It had better be quiet, as I told my nephew," Ethel said. "Billy cain't afford to lose his best renter, and that is me" she said.

"Is this guy at the motel really all that ugly, honey?"Mabel asked. "If he would clean hisself up a bit you could see if he wants any female company," Mabel said knowingly to Ethel.

"You took them words right outa my mouth, honey," Ethel said. "There ain't many bachelors his age in the county," she said as she chewed the apple pie.

"Beggars cain't be choosers," she had told herself when she saw

Carl's efforts at walking. "He needs someone to make sure he takes care of hisself," she had thought.

Carl, on his side, when he saw Ethel for the first time in the motel office talking to Billy, had felt completely neutral about his neighbor.

"She looks kinda like the first wife, and that is a bad sign," he had told himself.

Summer and Autumn passed quietly for Carl and his dogs. One Wednesday night at six o'clock he sat in the back of the Sunshine Market near the grill. The Sunshine had become a favorite hang out for him. They allowed dogs and on this night he had brought Buddy with him. The market was spare like everything else in the county. The concrete floors were not painted and the ceiling was unfinished. Wooden rafters with long aluminum joists hung overhead near the peaked roof of the building. Sundries, chips and candy were up front. Tonight locals who liked to sing and play their guitars met in the back for community music. Carl and Buddy sat and listened.

"The music tonight is so-so," thought Carl as he watched a middle-aged man in a sleeveless cotton shirt strum a guitar and then begin to drawl a country song.

The musician in question had several teeth missing and his eyes were red from too many nights spent at the tavern.

"His kind has seen better days," Carl reflected.

Next to the sleeveless musician sat a motley group of overweight and needy looking older men and women. Their instruments lay in their laps. A small, thin man and a very heavy older woman with her gray hair in a bun approached Carl and Buddy's table

"Needin company, stranger?" The woman said in a loud voice.

Without answering Carl slid a chair out from under the table toward her.

"Tommy, ain't he nice?" Mabel said. "Honey, here is yer chair. We will sit with this fella an his dog," she ordered looking over at her husband.

"You must be frum Calloway County or Ballard County," Mabel said looking into Carl's face.

"No, I am frum Montana," her company replied.

"That's a might fer from Kentucky. "They got all them big mountains out thar," Mabel said.

"They call it the "Big Sky Country," ma'am," Carl replied and then continued, "everything out there is big: the sky, the mountains and the prairie," he said.

While Carl spoke further about Montana, Mabel inspected him closely. He was short, paunchy and the legs stretched out from the chair in which he sat were bowed. He had heavy, western cowboy boots spotted with mud on his feet.

"How you like all the flat land and muddy streams hereabouts, stranger?" she asked him.

"I like it right fine," Carl said as he patted Buddy. "No one to bother me and my dogs at the Budget 6," he continued.

"Whut you need is a good womin to make you sit up straight in yer chair, honey," Mabel said in return.

"You look like a woman a man should not argue with, ma'am," Carl said looking from Tommy to Mabel.

"That's right honey, and my man Tommy here can vouch fer that," Mabel said smiling.

About that time the music became loud and the three companions and Buddy sat silently and listened to the music for the remainder of the evening.

Ethel stood sideways before her bureau mirror. It was late Friday evening a few weeks after Mabel and Tom had sat with Carl at the Sunshine Market. Her head was turned toward the mirror. She stared intently at herself.

"Not too bad fer sixty-one, but I don't wanna brag," she told herself. "There ain't any womin my age in the county ken come close to this ol gal," she thought as she looked at herself in the mirror.

She looked down at her legs, left bare by the pink shorts she was wearing.

"I allays had the legs," she thought. "The legs hadn't let me down like the ol bosom," she promised herself.

She then turned her body full length facing the mirror and bent forward at the waist with her face close to the glass, inspecting her eyebrows. She reached down on the bureau counter. Numerous plastic bottles and packages were strewn across its surface. Her still small and shapely fingers grabbed an eyebrow pencil. Her lips pursed tightly together and her face took on an intense seriousness. Carefully, she stenciled arching contours of color over the two brows above her clear blue eyes.

While Ethel was inspecting her appearance, Carl and his three animals were awake in their room. Bingo, the Chow, was no longer confined to his corner, and Buddy and Blaze had been brought from the vacant lot behind Budget 6 where they were sometimes leashed to a metal stake. Carl sat at the round table in the middle of the front room of his apartment with a stack of six barbecue sandwiches and two cans of beer on the table. Buddy and Blaze sat expectantly by his side eying the barbecue sandwiches as large portions disappeared into Carl's mouth. Barbecue sauce dripped from the corner of his mouth as he sat at an angle with his two legs spread before him. The phone rang and he picked up the receiver.

115.

"Hello," he answered over the sound of growling between Buddy and Blaze.

"Did you get the package I sent Monday?" A voice asked.

"Nope," Carl answered into the phone, recognizing his sister in Bozeman.

"I bet you did and just forgot," Wanda complained.

"No way, I am sharp as a tack," her brother said. "I don't forget nuthin," he promised.

"What did you do with the shoes I bought for you and mailed last month?" Wanda asked.

'Got em on right now," Carl said glancing over at the brown, tasseled loafers sitting in a box in the corner.

"Carl, I saw the most darlin blue and yellow rag sweater at the general store," his sister said. "It would be perfect for you," she said.

"Hangin up now sis," he said and put the receiver back in its cradle.

"Wanda is great," Carl thought to himself, "but she has control issues," he reflected.

Pulling off his heavy boots, he got up from the chair and walked in his soiled socks to the counter. The counter and adjacent sink were filled with dirty plates and glasses. Crumpled papers littered the floor, having fallen out of the plastic trash can.

After Carl's second divorce, he was a broken man. He had been fifty-eight years old when his second wife, Lydia, had filed the papers and left him. He had lived his entire life in Montana. As a young man he had managed very large loans from the Bank of Bozeman and then purchased a large tract of prime forest. Then, he had ruthlessly begun pursuing wealth in the timber industry. Carl was a man born with the knack of turning a profit. By the time he was in his early fifties he was one of the wealthiest and most influential men in Bozeman. His first marriage had been brief. He and Sally, his first wife, had met in high school and had married soon thereafter. Sally moved out after only eight months.

By age fifty-three, with the influence of money, Carl had married an upper class younger woman, Lydia. Lydia's father had been a mayor of Bozemen and was a prominent cattle rancher. Lydia had been educated at a prestigious university in California. She had returned to Bozeman to live off her father until she met and married Carl. During the five years of his second marriage Carl struggled to please his second wife. However, nothing was ever good enough for her. Their house was not sufficiently large nor opulent. Lydia would take frequent trips to Vancouver to shop for clothes and furniture. As his wife availed herself of the many things that Carl's money could buy, she gradually became less satisfied with Bozeman and with him. In the last year of their marriage, she met a wealthy, older man in Vancouver at an exclusive restaurant. That meeting eventually led to the end of her wish to stay married to Carl and the end of her satisfaction with life in Bozeman.

With the failure of his second marriage, the simple lumber magnate resolved to move where there were no bad memories and where he could be a stranger and outsider. In business he had no friends, and he was not a social person. When he was not working, he spent his time with his dogs. Other than pet ownership and the lumber business, his only interest was big game hunting. Soon, even elk season held no allure for him.

After Carl finished talking to Wanda on the phone, he spent a long time remembering things he had fought so hard to forget. He began to relive the pain that he hoped would fade, but never really did. He stood from his chair in his room of the motel and leaned down and started patting Blaze's long, shaggy coat. Bingo, the Chow, who normally stayed separate from the other two dogs walked over from his corner and sat in front of Carl, looking up at his master.

"Hot dogs, boys," the man said as his mood began to brighten. "This is no time for Purina; it's hot dog time," he repeated into the room.

If there was any thing that brightened Carl's mood, it was feeding time for the dogs. Opening the ice box by the sink, he took out three packages of frankfurters. He took his carbon steel, Case pocket knife from his britches and cut open the packages. Each dog: Buddy, Blaze and Bingo was given an entire package of cold wieners that was placed on the floor before them. As the three dogs gulped their meals, Carl knelt before them and gave each one a hearty hug.

Carl and the little dog, Buddy, stood before their apartment door at the Budget 6. It was ten o'clock on a Monday night The solitary street light across the parking lot on US 45 did a poor job of lighting the front side of the motel. Carl and Buddy had just arrived back from a night of country music at the Sunshine Market. Carl fumbled with his key and put it into the door lock. The door squeaked on its hinges and then swung open as he pushed it back. Stepping inside the door jam followed by Buddy, he switched on the light. Blaze lay near the door looking up with one-third of the skin of his face ripped off, raw and bloody. The chairs near the table lay on their sides and the plastic trash can was turned over and empty. Trash was scattered all about the room. In the back of the room Carl could see Bingo, the Chow, sitting looking at the occupants inside the doorway. Bingo's muzzle was colored a bright red.

"Yer goin back in solitary, buster, Carl muttered to Bingo as he entered the room , followed by Buddy.

Despite the fact that Blaze had been injured in an apparent fight with Bingo the night before, Carl slept late. However, he slept fitfully, this being his usual mode of resting at night. He had a long history of insomnia. During that night he awakened about two in the morning. Bingo, the Chow, had been chained near the bath-room. Blaze and Buddy slept at the side of his bed. Carefully, he swung his legs over the two sleeping dogs near the bed as he got up. Upon standing from a lying position his mind spun in circles. He put his right hand upon the mattress to steady himself. Managing to cross the room with the aid of the streetlight through the half closed blinds, he ambled to the sink and drew a glass of water. The tap water at the Budget 6 was cloudy with particulates from the pipes and it had the strong taste of chlorine. Soon, he was back lying on the mattress and "out" for the rest of the night.

At ten o'clock that morning, he roused himself from sleep. He led the injured Blaze on a leash to the front office of the Budget 6. Billy and Ethel were in the office at the time. As Carl and Blaze entered, Ethel who was at the register, could see the damage to the dog's head. By this time the bare skin was crusted over with patches of dark, clotted blood. A thin stream of bright red trickled down from the corner of Blaze's right eye and dripped from his muzzle onto the floor creating a small puddle of blood.

"Billy, come over here and see whut has happened next door" Ethel said with alarm.

Her nephew walked over and stood beside the counter, looking but not speaking. Ethel at once walked around the corner, grabbing a wet cloth from a drawer, and knelt before Blaze.

As she began washing the face of the injured animal, Blaze struggled to get away.

"Hold still, mister," Carl said emphatically, and he grabbed the leash holding it a few inches from Blaze's neck. He knelt down near his sixty-one year old female neighbor.

"You should be ashamed of yerself letting yer dogs fight like this," she said angrily to Carl as she struggled to help Blaze.

"Whut do I need with shame, lady?" Carl asked. "Shame ain't gonna put skin back on a dog's head where it has been torn off,"

119.

he said testily.

"Honey, this doggy is goin to the vet, and I am gonna take him right now," Ethel cried wresting the leash from Carl's grasp.

The Montana lumberman was taken aback, but he was not in the mood to confront his feisty neighbor. He followed her and the injured Blaze to a rusted-out green Volkswagen bus and climbed into the back seat after Blaze was installed in the rear. Ethel manned the driver's seat.

Three hours later Ethel, Carl, and Blaze drove back to the Budget 6. Blaze had received an antibiotic shot and a pain killer. His injured head had been cleaned with antiseptic. Blaze now sat in the back seat. The two humans were in front.

"Billy has tol me you'all are frum Montana," Ethel said.

"I ain't got nuthin keepin me back there," the laconic Carl replied.

"Uh, huh, better fer a young lady not to ask questions, I see," she said. "My friend Mabel and her Tommy seen you at the Sunshine a few weeks ago," Ethel said.

"She tol me whut I need is a good womin to make me sit up straight when I have company," Carl said.

"A good womin, friend, will let you sit any way that you like," Ethel replied cautiously.

"I don't want to insult a female, but I have only known women who were nuthin but trouble," he said.

Ethel decided, at that point, no to pursue the topic of men-women relationships further She put out her right hand and gently patted Carl on his thigh.

120.

"The way to a man's heart is through his stomach, honey," Mabel said to Ethel as the two women sat in Mabel's kitchen on yet another Sunday afternoon.

"When I was a youngin, I had no problem gettin fellas, but things have changed," Ethel complained.

"Didn't yer Billy say that this particular fella is loaded?" Mabel asked.

"That is whut he said, but you know Billy: he don't know nuthin," her friend replied.

"Well, honey, you ken take care of yourself. You don't need an old man's money," the host related.

Ethel reached over and picked up la big piece of German chocolate cake. As she chewed the moist cake she looked up and said, "give me the recipe of this cake, honey."

Two weeks later, Ethel spent Friday evening baking a German chocolate cake. She had bought the ingredients days before. Although Ethel had considerable experience with boyfriends, she was nervous the night she made the cake. Never having married, she was not the proficient cook that Mabel was. All went well with the cooking, and by ten p.m. the cake was out of the oven and on top of the stove. She waited until the cake was cool and then generously applied the icing, making swirls in it as she applied it onto the cake top with a large spoon. Putting the finished cake into a box, she went to bed.

At nine a.m. the next morning Ethel was dolled up and standing before the door to Carl's apartment. She knocked on the door. Few things were private in such a small motel. Carl had recognized her dress through a gap in his front curtains as she stood knocking at his door. There was no answer. Not one to be easily dissuaded from a task at hand, she began knocking forcefully. Finally, she put the cake down before the door on the sidewalk and stalked away.

121.

Back in her darkened room, she sank into a chair, despondent. Her
eyes filled with tears.

"Don't that man know whut is good fer him?" she thought with exasperation. "He needs a womin like me worse than any man I ever
met," she said. Then she began tearing a paper napkin into small
shreds and thew the shreds onto the floor at her feet.

Soon she fell into an uneasy sleep, upright in her chair with her
chin forward on her breast, snoring softly. She awoke later that
evening and everything about her was dark. She raised her head
from her breast and looked at the unwashed cooking utensils laying
on the counter. Despite the many men in her life, Ethel was not a
stranger to disappointment. As a young beauty, she had never felt
desperate for companionship. She felt desperate now.

 "Is this going to be the rest of my life?" She asked herself. "Ain't
nuthin good comin into my life anymore?" She wondered.

The next morning, after she left the German chocolate cake at
Carl's door, she noticed that it was gone. Three days later, she still
had not seen any sign of her bachelor neighbor nor his animals. In
reality, she had been going out early and coming home late to avoid
seeing Carl and his animals anyway.

"Maybe he just was not able to come out and get the cake when
I was knocking that morning," she had thought. "I know the man
woulda liked the cake if'n he ate any of it," she told herself.

Several weeks later, Ethel was sitting alone in her room looking out
the curtains. She was still trying to catch a glimpse of her neighbor.
It was three p.m. when her impatience got the better of her. She
rose from her couch, exited her apartment and walked briskly to the
front office. As was his habit, Billy was lounging in a metal chair
behind the cash register.

122.

"Whur is he, honey?" she asked Billy.

'Whur is who?" Billy replied.

"That ol man with the three mangy dogs. I ain't seen them in the longest time," she complained.

"He's gone...Moved out a while ago," Billy said glumly.

"Where'd he go then, Billy...Did he say?" She asked.

"Hell, no. He just clean left one morning early. Here lookit this," and Billy shoved a check into here face. "He left this check on the desk here and overpaid his rent by one hundred dollars, but there was no note nor nuthin," her nephew said.

123.

Part Two

It was late February, two months since Carl had checked out of the Budget 6 motel. Ethel was at the front desk that afternoon. A late model, red Chevy Camaro pulled up to the motel, blowing smoke out of the tailpipe. The bright red paint was chipped in places, showing years of wear. A muscular young man, about thirty-five years old walked inside. At first glance, Ethel was suspicious. She had seen a Georgia license plate hanging loosely from the front end of the sport car. The man had a clear complexion with thick lips and short blonde hair brushed to stand on end with hair gel. He had a coarse look about him. He looked at Ethel.

"Gotta room for two?" he asked.

"I see you, honey, where's the two?" Ethel asked.

"Baby, get in here," Bubba called over his shoulder.

The front passenger door to the Camaro opened and a woman walked inside the motel.

"This gal in nuthin but cheap," Ethel thought.

Cindy's head came up to her companion's shoulder. Bubba was over six feet in height, Cindy was five foot two inches tall. Her light brown hair was shoulder length and straight. As she stopped at the desk beside the man, her pink lips spread into a smile.

"This here's my babe. She's my number two," the blonde man said looking straight at Ethel.

"Bubba, baby, I need me sum rest," the young woman said plaintively.

She was young, but had a womanly figure: she was curvy in all the right places. Ethel grimaced as she filled out the order for their room.

124.

"Gotta room, be ready in twenty minutes," Ethel said adjusting her reading glasses on her face.

As the man and woman left to wait for their room, Ethel watched with disapproval as Cindy's rounded rear exited through the office door.

Earlier, in January, Frank and Sam sat in their office at the REMAX Realty on a cold morning. Outside their office window the snow came down in flurries. The normally muddy front yard was frozen. Gray trees outlined the view across the road. Inside, the office was small and old. Its walls were covered in cheap, pine paneling. Faded white acoustic tiles hung from the ceiling. The desk in the office was a reconditioned gray metal desk, left over from the bankruptcy of another local business. The two large swivel chairs had brown plastic seats.

"I cain't believe the one hundred acres of land down at Leder Bottoms finally sold," Frank said into the air as his face tilted upward.

"Dan has been tryin to sell that land fer years now," Sam acknowledged." "Who the hell took all one hundred acres off his hands?" Sam asked Frank."

"Well, the man looked pretty broken down, and I ain't seen his likes before," Frank said. "You ken write a check for the land, but you won't get no land until it clears," I tol him. "Dammit, his check cleared that same week," Frank said.

Sam stood up from his chair and walked over to a corner. He poured himself a cup of coffee from a metal coffee pot sitting on an electric hot plate. His oversized stomach projected beyond a cracked black leather belt. A red and green striped tie hung loosely around his neck.

"This guy with the big check, he probly got his money in sum sinful place like Las Vega or sum other such place," Sam said with dis-

125.

gust.

"Yer right, brother," Frank agreed. "Whur did he say he wuz from?"
Frank asked.

"The check wuz from Bozeman, Montana, but it's no tellin where
that bum is really frum," Sam said.

"You gotta watch a stranger like him," Frank continued. "If you don't
watch'em close, they will rob you blind and stab you in the back at
the same time," he said.

After Carl moved out of the Budget 6, he and his three dogs lived
in his car until the check cleared at REMAX. Their new home was
one hundred acres of marsh land near the swamp of Leder Bottoms. In the center of the Bottoms was a slowly flowing stream of
muddy water filled with catfish and chubs. The marsh and swamp of
Leder Bottoms had never been farmed because the land would not
support the weight of a tractor or other heavy equipment. Hence, it
had all lain fallow. A narrow graveled road led to his property, five
miles off US 45 which ran between Lone Oak and Mayfield.

Leder Bottoms was on the line between McCracken and Graves
Counties in Western Kentucky. This area was a no-man's land.
Few people lived here. On Carl's one hundred acres a two-bed-
room, modular house sat fifty feet back from the road. A dirt drive
led from the graveled road to the side of the house and then continued back through a field to a barbed wire fence. An unpainted metal gate in the fence gave access to a weathered chicken coop and
rabbit hutch. When Carl, Bingo, Buddy and Blaze moved into the
property it had been abandoned for six years. The nearest neigh-
bors were the Cooper family, who lived two miles further down the
graveled road off US 45.

Two weeks after the sale of the one hundred acres in Leder Bottoms, Sam drove down to the place to retrieve his REMAX sign. As
he pulled his car onto the dirt drive, he noticed white sheets hung

on the front windows to block the sunlight. The front of the house faced an easterly direction.

"I guess this guy likes to sleep late," he said to himself as he knocked loudly without an answer. He walked around to the back of the house. The backyard was barren with just a few patches of dried brown grass in the dirt. Hearing noises from insided the chicken coop, he walked inside the coop through its open door. Sam saw Carl bent over spreading cracked corn from a bucket onto the cold ground. Twenty Bantam chickens pecked furiously at the corn.

"How're you likin her new place, neighbor?" The realtor said in a friendly tone of voice.

"It's just whut me and the dogs were needin. Why are you askin?" Carl replied standing up and looking at his visitor.

"Ain't many folks ken take livin our here with soy bean fields on one side of em and swamp on t'other," Sam replied.

"Sum of the local farmers have stopped by for a talk to keep things frum gettin too lonely," Carl said.

"Which ones, ken I ask?" Sam said.

Carl rubbed his hands together, to shake the dust from the corn off and said, "there's the ol farmer, W.E. Bell and his son R.S. Bell for starters."

"Honest family men," Sam said.

"You ain't gonna find better no-where," Carl advised.

"Come on inside and I'll fix you a little somethin fer yer stummich afor you go," Carl offered.

"Thanky, I will," his visitor said.

127.

Ten minutes later, the two men sat in plain wooden chairs before the old stove in the kitchen. A large pot of white beans was cooking, and before them on a table were two bowls of the beans, a bottle of red ketchup and glasses of tea. Sam entertained Carl with the history of soybean farming in Western Kentucky. The large fields between the one hundred acres and the four-way stop near the Budget 6 would be planted in the coming Spring and harvested with a combine in the Fall. The realtor followed this topic with details of Mr. Bell and his son and their many relatives. All of these people now lived in Mayfield, fifteen miles on the south side of the Bottoms.

The February day Bubba and Cindy moved into their room at the Budget 6, Ethel answered the phone.

"Honey, my man Tom has found yer mystery man," Mabel said excitedly over the phone line.

"I tol you how he wouldn't come to his door in January, and how he moved his sorry ass outa his room. Why should I care about a beat up loser like him?" Ethel remarked.

"He ain't no loser, honey," her friend quickly said. "That stranger paid fer one hundred acres and a house in Leder Bottoms with cash money a few days after he ran off frum you," Mabel exclaimed.

"How did ol Tom find his where-abouts?" Ethel asked.

"Tom says this guy has been at the Saturday horse auction all Win-ter," Mabel replied.

"You ought to know , honey, that this ol gal has allays been horse crazy," Ethel spewed out.

"Whut are you a'doin this Saturday night?" Mabel asked.

That week Billy and Ethel sat in the front office. Cindy walked in at noon. Her hair had been mussed during the night and she had hastily pulled it back with bobby pins. Stray strands of soft brown hair hung around her neck. A midriff length, yellow knit sweater revealed ample regions of her midsection above tight-fitting Span-dex leotards. Billy, who was standing at the cash register, did not speak. His eyes were fixed on a gold ring which had been pierced to her navel. A knowing smile clung to Cindy's lips as she looked at Ethel. The older woman glared. Suddenly, Ethel pushed her neph-ew away from the cash register and took his place.

"How far is it to the nearest take-out, baby," Cindy said looking over at Billy and ignoring Ethel. "My bubba is hungry, honey," she con-tinued.

Billy   stammered a reply as his mind whirled with thoughts of what might have happened in their room during the night.

"They's a fried chickin place north of here three miles," he said. "I bet yer a killer in the kitchen when you've a mind to be," he then said eagerly.

"Ain't you sweet, baby," Cindy said, "and yer right, I kin whup up a mean skillet when I put my little mind to it," she finished. Then she turned her back on him and left the office.

It was a cold February afternoon and the wind had been bitter that day. Carl looked through the boards of a circular corral, built by two local men he had met at the farm supply. His arms were propped on the top rail as he leaned against the fence watching his new gelding within the paddock. He had purchased Jesse at the horse auctions the previous week. Jesse walked up to Carl while Blaze sat at Carl's side-man and dog on the outer side of the fence. The red gelding's large head reached over for the apple that was held out to him. Jesse was a small horse, about fourteen hands high. His conformation was stocky. He had the thick neck and powerful hindquarters of a quarter horse. When Carl had seen the gelding exercising in the show ring at the auction, he knew this was the an-imal for him. Despite being gelded, Jesse was high-spirited. Carl liked the rusty red color of Jesse's coat. Before being sold, the horse had run wild on an old farm. Jesse had never been ridden.

Saturday night, the seats at the horse auction were cold and hard.

"I thought you said Tom saw that guy here," Ethel complained to Mabel after the two women had been sitting for one hour.

By the time they had arrived at six that evening, seating was scarce.

"Jus like sum man not be here at the right time," Mabel commiserated with her friend.

"They ain't got no sense, no how, honey," Ethel said.

Mabel had arthritis in her spine and as the night at the auction wore on, the pain got worse. She leaned forward over her large stomach, putting her hands beside her on the bench to relieve the stress on her back.

"Nobody gonna talk to us with you lookin like that, honey," Ethel related.

Finally, at ten o'clock the two women were walking through the crowded parking lot toward Mabel's truck.

"I cain't believe my eyes. There's his blue and white station wagon," Ethel whispered.

Curious, she grabbed Mabel by the coat and pulled her over to the car.

"They's them ugly dogs," Ethel said excitedly. Blaze, Buddy and Bingo were in the back of the wagon.

"Well, honey, we cain't wait fer a man we hardly know standin at his car," Mabel said emphatically. "We two look like a coupla female stalkers," she explained.

"He ain't worth it no how," Ethel replied.

The two rural women walked back to Mabel's truck. Ethel felt her heart sinking. She struggled to keep tears from collecting in her eyes, not wanting to let Mabel see how upset she was.

"Cat got yer tongue, honey," Mabel complained later in the truck driving back to Ethel's apartment. "You ain't said nuthin fer thirty minutes," she related. Ethel sat silently in the front passenger seat.

After Carl and his dogs moved into their single story home in Leder Bottoms, he began fixing up the place. Originally just a house with a chicken coop and rabbit hutch, the place now had a rough shod paddock and a four stall stables for the quarter horse. Carl had purchased a number of Bantam hens and a single Bantam rooster, but so far he had no rabbits. Being from Montana, Carl was some-what familiar with horses, although he had never personally owned one.

"You get yerself straw fer to cover the ground of the stalls, and you need hay fer him to eat," W.E. Bell had explained one night in Carl's kitchen.

W.E. was a retired soybean farmer, and in appearance, was a male version of Ethel's friend Mabel. Sitting in a chair over a large pot of beef stew, W.E.'s stomach extended well beyond his skinny legs and chest.

"I don't know how this guy ken walk with his belly stickin out so far," Carl had thought to himself.

To maintain his robust size, W.E. really packed away the food when he was at Carl's table. The ex-lumberman kept the Kentucky farm-er's plate well-filled during their visits.

Late one morning after an early visit by W.E., Carl's station wagon pulled into his dirt drive at ten o'clock. The back of the wagon was filled with purchases from the farm supply. Although Carl walked slowly and with a limp, his chest and arms were strong. After a few quick trips between the car and the stables, a bale of straw, a bale of hay and a large bag of whole oats were thrown into the back of one of the four stalls. The stables had not been painted; Carl let the oak boards weather naturally. With Jesse tied up in the first stall, Carl grabbed a long-handle spade and mucked out the remaining empty stalls. He lay straw down in one cleaned out stall and put Jessee into it. He filled a steel tub with water and watched his horse drink. Then he filled a nose bag with whole oats and tied in onto the horse's head.

Back in his house, he lay down on a steel cot in the bedroom and began to sleep. That evening he awakened to the ring of the rotary phone in the kitchen.

"Git in yer car and meet me at the mile 67 marker on US 45 partner," W.E. said into Carl's ear.

"Ain't it late in the day fer that?" Carl asked.

"They's an abandoned green Volkswagen bus on the side of the road there, and we need to check it out," W.E. answered.

It was six miles from Carl's house to mile marker 67. The stretch of road was desolate and the weather was inhospitable that day. If someone was alone in the car, it could be the next day before anyone discovered them. The blue and white station wagon with Carl in the driver's seat made its way toward mile marker 67. Evening was fast approaching, and a northerly wind whipped about his car.

Nearing the green vehicle, Carl could see W.E.'s truck with it rusted, metal rails bolted to the bed of the pickup. The farmer was standing near the driver side door of the green car. Carl parked his wagon and approached his friend.

"You need to come outa there, lady. I don't mean no harm," he heard W.E. say in a voice raised above the wind.

"How long you been here?" Carl asked W.E., standing at the car.

132.

"I been here too long fer a lady who don't talk and who won't get herself outa this here car," the farmer complained.

The man from Montana peered through the dirty driver's side window to see Ethel sitting at the wheel with her eyes looking straight ahead and avoiding W.E.

After Carl saw Ethel sitting in the front seat, he tapped W.E. on the shoulder.

"Give me a shot at this," he said.

He walked to his wagon and got a large wrench from the toolbox that he kept in the back of the wagon. He walked to the green car, standing at the side nearest the road. He leaned his head and face across the windshield so Ethel could clearly see him and began rapping loudly on the glass. Suddenly, the driver side door opened and its female occupant emerged.

"Yer gonna break the glass," Ethel shouted as Carl turned to face her.

"You been plannin on walkin the ten mile back to the Budget 6?" He asked with a forced smile.

Seeing Carl before her, Ethel's mood softened. Her tone became gracious.

"I bet a big strong man like you ken fix anything a poor female needs fixin," she said.

"Let me git my toolbox. You pop the hood and then you ken sit back inside yer car," he said to her.

After the hood was opened and propped up, the Montana man went about his business. After about twenty minutes, he forcefully closed the hood and walked over to the driver's side window which has half lowered.

133.

"Try it now," he suggested.

Turning her key in the ignition, the car gave a few halting noises and the front end began to shake.

"Well, honey...You did yer best," Ethel said while Carl stood by.

She got out of the Volkswagen and stood by her attempted helper.

"I'll take a lift back to my place frum a good lookin fella like you...if'n you are offerrin," she said looking directly into his eyes.

W. E., who had been watching all the time spoke, "you go on and take this womin back home Carl. I am headin back to my house," he said. W.E. then climbed into the cab of his truck and cranked up his engine.

Fifteen minutes of silence ensued as Carl drove Ethel back to the Budget 6. Although she didn't speak during this time, she noticed the bad condition of the wagon. In front of her, the hatch to the glove compartment hung open. A stack of unused white napkins lay haphazardly inside. She reached a hand forward and tried to close the glove compartment, but its latch was broken and the hatch fell open again. At her feet, a light layer of dust covered the floor mat. To her right, the passenger-view window was streaked. The air in the wagon was uncomfortably hot, and the fan blew with a rattle.

It was dark when Carl and Ethel pulled into the parking lot of the motel. Carl pulled the wagon up to the door of the office. The light inside was on. Opening the door and once on her feet and out of the car, Ethel tried to speak, but Carl held up his hand.

'You don't need to thank me; it's me that owes you. That cake you made fer me was the best if ever et," he said through the car window.

The sixty-one year old woman replied, "if'n you want another cake, you know where you ken find me," she said and then walked inside.

The morning after Carl dropped Ethel off at the motel, she awoke to find her green car in the motel parking lot.

"I don't know how he dun it this fast, but why should I care about how it wuz dun," she told Billy as they sat together that day in the motel office.

"That ol bum is loaded," Billy muttered.

"Honey, keep yer trap shut," she told her nephew, "word might get back to him. I don't care whut he looks like now; I think he will clean up right fine," she bragged.

Ethel then looked up from her conversation with Billy, only to see Cindy and Bubba standing before them.

"You got yerself a honey?" Cindy asked Ethel.

"Hell ya, baby," Bubba exclaimed, "I think she's caught herself a live one," he said in a loud voice.

'If'n you two don't keep yer mouths shut about all this, I am throwin ya'll out," Ethel said between clenched teeth.

Billy watched as Cindy's little fingers played with a silver necklace hanging just above her bodice.

"You seein anything you like, baby?" she asked him softly.

"Honey, they all like you; you know that," Bubba said with a grin.

Then Bubba slapped Billy on the shoulder.

"It don't hurt to look, ol man; but don't think of touchin," he said.

"Billy, get me a bucket of water, I need to mop this dirty office,"

Ethel said abruptly.

"The bucket is rusted and I threw it away last month," he com-plained.

"Get yerself down to the farm supply and get another one," she advised her nephew firmly.

Thirty minutes later, Billy returned to the motel with a bucket, but Cindy and Bubba had left by then.

Saturday morning was a time that Ethel spent shopping. During the week, she was often needed in the front office of the motel. Billy staffed the office on Saturday. It was nine-thirty a.m. on a Satur-day, and Ethel found herself at the ladies dress shop in Mayfield. As she walked the aisles, she noticed the young shop girl follow-ing her. Ignoring the shop girl, Ethel halted and picked up a red, crepe dress from the rack. She held the wire hanger in one hand and draped the dress over the other hand. The fabric was soft and yielding.

"I need something to show off , whut I got," she thought to herself.

"This rack of clothes is twenty percent off, ma'am," the young girl mentioned, trying to catch Ethel's eye.

Ethel looked over, frowning.

"I don't need no discount, honey," she said.

Ethel looked down at her faded jeans and she looked at her black shoes with prominent brown faded spots in the heels. Ethel put the dress back on the rack, and fingered the buttons on the front of her white blouse. She turned and walked to the next aisle, and the girl followed her.

Grabbing several large plastic, blue spangles for her arms, she walked toward the check-out at a brisk pace. Looking into the face of the girl as her order was rung up, she took out a fifty dollar bill and handed it over.

"I 'll be back next week fer the purty dress. Ken you keep it back til then?" She asked.

"Of course ma'am, and please take your time and look around further," the girl said eagerly.

Back in her room at the Budget 6, Ethel searched her closet and brought out a small cardboard box. She took several fifty dollar bills out and tucked them into her change purse, before putting the box back. She walked over to the mirror and began inspecting herself.

"That purty red dress is just right," she thought, while raising her eyebrows and picking up a mascara stick.

She doused her eyelashes with a heavy dose of mascara.

"I don't need no rouge," she said under her breath, "I got natural blush in my cheeks."

137.

Part Three

It was now four months after Ethel's car broke down on US 45. The time of the year was late June. Carl had been absent from Ethel's life, but he had been busy. In the morning he collected eggs from the Bantam hens and placed them in a bowl on the kitchen table. His usual breakfast was corn flakes in milk or scrambled eggs and toast. After collecting the eggs at dawn and feeding the three dogs, he made his way to the stables. There he saw to it that Jesse had plenty of oats, hay and water. Leading the stocky horse from his stall by a long leader rope, he exercised him in the paddock. Jesse had learned to run the circle around his owner on the leader rope. Carl stood in the center of the paddock with a leather switch in his hand to keep Jesse at a brisk trot.

One night Carl sat in his rocker listening to the black, plastic radio on the counter. The night outside was blustery and wet. He could hear the wind as it whistled through the vertical cracks between the boards of the stables. The thud, thud of Jesse's hooves on the boards of his stall reached his ears. As he was dozing off, he heard the phone ring.

"Yep," he answered.

"How old are you gonna get afore you find yourself a girlfriend?" His sister, Wanda, asked.

"Bout the time you find yerself a rich husband," Carl answered back.

"You know I have sworn off the opposite sex, brother, but you don't have to follow my example," Wanda replied. "Aren't there any nice women in the flat and dusty land of Western Kentucky?" She asked him.

"Well, sis, there is the gal that made me that German chocolate cake. She ain't bad lookin if'n I do say so mysell," he said raising his voice with interest.

"There you go, honey. You get yourself over to her place and do something about it before you are six feet under," Wanda ordered.

Like most bachelors, Carl did more dreaming and wishing than he did gettin up out of his chair and doing. And like many men in his sixties, he needed a push to get going. Wanda was the one to do the pushing, and she usually got her way. As the weeks of living between soybean fields and the marshes of Leder Bottoms wore on, Carl had been thinking about Ethel. When he considered approaching her at the Budget 6, his mind became a jumble of conflicting thoughts.

I was not until the middle of July that Carl pulled his blue and white wagon into the Budget 6 lot. The three dogs were not in the back of the wagon on this day. The back of the wagon was filled with old shirts. It was the afternoon, and like any other afternoon in July, the air was muggy and oppressive. He got out of the car, went to the rear and opened the tailgate. He gathered the faded and wrinkled shirts together. Walking into the front office with the shirts, he met the tall and thin Billy.

"Whur you come frum, neighbor?" Billy asked looking up from a magazine with a white-skinned model straddling an oversized motorcycle on its cover.

"I am in need of somethin only a woman ken do," Carl said.

"That covers alot of territory, friend," Billy replied.

The hotel manager the picked up the phone and rang his aunt.

"I have a fella here who needs a womin," he said into the receiver.

Ethel thought a moment as she listened to Billy.

"There ain't no man on this green Earth that don't need a womin," she said.

139.

"Come on into the front office and see whut I mean," Billy requested and then he put down the phone.

Ethel walked into the office. Hearing her enter, Carl turned around with his arms full of shirts.

"You needin a real woman or a maid?" She asked as she looked at him.

Carl remained silent.

"No matter , honey," she said softening her tone and taking the shirts into her possession.

"My dear if'n these shirts don't need help with a needle and thread," she said.

"I ken fix these tears, but you are gonna do yer own washing and ironing," she concluded.

"I would be much obliged ma'am. I am not in the habit of askin fer a lady's number," he said as he took a pencil from his pocket and scribbled a note on a piece of paper. With a worried look in his eyes, he handed the paper to Ethel.

"Well, honey, you are the only fella I would give my number to," she said and she quickly wrote her own note and handed it to Carl. "When the shirts are done, honey, you will know," she said and gathered up the shirts and left .

Ethel stood before Mabel in her friend's country kitchen. Mabel gave out a long whistle and then said, "come on in here Tom and take a look it yer wife's friend."

"Whoa...if'n she don't look fine," Tom said as he walked into the room

Ethel smiled with pride as she smoothed out the fabric of a red dress with her hands. The red skirt fell at her knees, showing the well-kept calves and thighs of the sixty-one year old woman. The blouse was gathered at her slender waist and it draped attractively from her shoulders.

"Now, honey, how long are you gonna take with that man's shirts?" Mabel queried.

"'I need sum time to let him see me in this dress first," Ethel answered.

"Yer gonna have to catch him out somewhere besides that muddy mess where he is a'livin honey," Mabel conveyed.

"I got the rest of my life to do that, honey. No other womin is gonna give him a second look livin out in the Bottoms," Ethel said. "I gotta clear playin field," she said excitedly.

With Ethel, Carl knew that he was entering new territory. He had never had a successful relationship with a woman before. It had been two weeks since he had left his shirts at the motel.

"I think she has had enough time now," he told himself one night while he sat in the kitchen in the rocker.

By this time, eight o'clock, he was tired from the day's activities. He had made his rounds that morning, taking care of the animals. The three dogs were in the house with him. Fortunately, there had been nor more fighting between Bingo and the two other dogs since the night in the motel. Carl looked over at the Chow laying in the corner of the kitchen. Blaze and Buddy lay by the rocking chair.

Earlier that afternoon, Carl had spent some time repairing a fence on his land. He had dug several post holes and put new fence posts in the ground. Then he had used a wire-stretcher to give tautness to the wire fencing between the new posts. He knew not to put the fence repair off until the Autumn when the ground might be hardened by the cold. Carl's land, like the adjoining soybean fields was flat. It was covered in sage grass.

"Some day I am gonna plant fescue on my land," he had thought. "I think they's folks around here needin the fescue to feed their cattle and horses," he reflected. "I ken get W.E.'s son R.S. to cut and bale it, and I could hold back enough to feed Jesse," he thought.

The stables had plenty of spare room to store bales of hay. Over-all, the physical labor of the farm helped keep his spirits up. That is, until the evening set in and it was just he and the dogs in the house.

Eying the rotary phone on the table beside him that night, he picked up the receiver and dialed Ethel's number. Ethel had just finished washing her hair. In her lap was a paper sack of popped micro-wave popcorn. Her phone rang.

"Is that you, Mabel?" She said into the receiver.

No one spoke.

"Well, I cain't believe my oldest friend has nuthn to say after ringing me this time of the night," Ethel said.

"It ain't Mabel," a voice suddenly said.

"Well, it's my disappearing , ex-neighbor, aint it honey?" Ethel asked loudly.

"Whut's goin on with my shirts?" Carl said gruffly.

"Don't you know how to talk to a lady?" Ethel retorted. "I am a'thinkin you better be real polite, if'n you want an answer," she advised him.

"Sorry, neighbor lady, I haven't called a womin in years, " Carl said meekly.

"That's better, honey...Sugar is better'n salt," Ethel said with satisfaction. "Well, Mr. Carl Trep...I am a'headin yer way tomorrow morning. Whut time will you be ready to meet me?" She asked.

The next morning the July weather was complicated by thunder showers.

"I don't care whut the sky does today. I am a'takin this man his shirts," she had told Mabel that morning over the phone.

The shirts had actually been finished for some time, but Ethel had been putting off a meeting with Carl at his home. Despite her prior warning to him that she was no maid, she not only had mended the shirts, but washed and pressed them. Then she neatly folded them and put them into boxes tied with colored twine.

It was a long drive from the motel to the graveled road off US 45. By ten o'clock she was standing on his porch, boxes of shirts in hand. When Carl opened the door, he was surprised to see Ethel dressed in an attractive, red dress. Loosely draped over her shoulders was a short rain jacket with the front open.

"How long has it been, honey, since you have had company?" She asked as she walked past him.

"It's been a right long while," he answered.

Carl then followed her as she walked toward the kitchen and put the boxes of shirts down on the table.

"If'n I am a'drivin all the way out here, I ain't goin back until I sit a spell," she informed him.

Ethel pulled up a chair and sat down with the back of the chair to the kitchen table. She faced Carl's rocker. He slowly sat down in the rocker facing her, and they looked at one another.

"He's cleaned hisself up a bit," she reflected as she looked him over.

143.

His white hair had been cut and parted neatly on the left. His face
was shaven, and he had a clean blue and black, checkered shirt
neatly buttoned. He wore a pair of clean blue jeans. As Ethel
looked at him, she noticed that he didn't seem happy.

"They's a sad look in his grey eyes," she reflected.

"I have your number, Ethel," he said quietly.

"Yes, Carl and you and I don't have time to waste," she replied.

At that point he smiled.

"There ain't much to do hereabouts, Ethel, he said.

"Well, honey, they's talkin and eatin and talkin sum more," she
said. "We can do that anytime we've a mind to," she suggested.

"I would like that," he said. "Now, would you like a cup of coffee?"
He asked her.

144.

Bobby

It was evening. Outside the windows of Value Market the night was
descending. The weather had been cold for weeks. The October
skies had become slate-gray, but now were a dense black. Bobby was at the front of the store visiting with the few women who
worked the evening shift. His best friend, Shorty, was cleaning
up in the butcher shop. Bobby was still in school. Shorty had
dropped out two years before. Shorty had a girlfriend. Shorty was
Irish; he had the "gift of the gab." He also had the Irish nose, and
the blonde hair and fair complexion of many Irish.

Veronica was Bobby's favorite check-out-girl, and she was working
tonight. Veronica had vivid red hair and a sharp tongue, but she
was the best checker at Value Market. Her register never came up
short of money at night. Just before closing time, Bobby stood at
Veronica's stand. A thin, needy-looking old man in baggy jeans was
checking out. His pants were half-unzipped and the strong odor of
liquor clung to him. He slurred his words, Barely managing to get
the needed cash from his wallet, he paid for a salami and stumbled
toward the door. Once this man was outside, Mr. Wallace came
down from his office and locked the front doors.

Value Market was situated across from the projects in Greenville.
The clientele who shopped there were poor. Mr. Wallace was the
only independent grocer who was still in business, since the large
chain-groceries had moved into town. After closing, Bobby and
Shorty walked the female employees to their cars. Although the
large, square parking lot was well-lit, it still was not safe. Tonight,
Bobby escorted Veronica to her old Chevrolet. Usually, the talkative Veronica would review the day's highlights as she was walked
to her car. Tonight, they were both silent. As the single woman
opened the driver's side door to her car, she reached down and
pressed something into Bobby's hand. The young man opened
his hand, and was surprised to find a bright-green five dollar bill.
To Bobby, who made a dollar-fifty an hour, the five dollar bill was a
happening.

145.

Bobby lived at home, but he was not there much. What little time he spent at his parent's house, he was usually asleep. He had been self-supporting since age fifteen. He was now nineteen, working his way through Northeast State Community College. His dream was to be an electrical technician and then to move as far away from his hometown as he could get. He avoided his parents, especially his father. Once Bobby had reached the age of fifteen, he had been thrust into a forbidding adult world. If he was to make it, he had to do it all by himself. His father, according to his own friends, was a "hard ass." His mother was a quiet woman and Bobby knew little about her. When she wasn't cooking and clean-ing, she spent her time in her bedroom reading. Bobby could never remember experiencing affection from his parents. His memory was only good back to age five. Before that, he could not remem-ber how he had been treated.

Bobby drove a 65 Ford. His father had sold him the car at age sixteen for five-hundred dollars. After six months of ownership, the car's engine went out and Bobby took three-hundred dollars of his clerk's salary and had a rebuilt engine put into his car. He was not surprised when his father seemed completely uninterested in the fact that he had sold a piece of junk to his unsuspecting son. Bob-by knew, after all, that all the old man was really interested in was another five-hundred dollars in his own pocket. The Ford was the only real property that the clerk owned. Every Sunday, he parked it in the front lawn of his parent's house and washed and waxed it. The only thing Bobby did not like about his car was that it did not have air conditioning. After he had put the re-built engine into the car, he saved enough money for a paint job. He replaced the dull enamel paint for acrylic.

The Value Market was bustling. It was Saturday afternoon, and the warmth inside the store was interrupted by a chill wind down the front aisle as the shoppers came and went through the front door. Mr. Wallace and his wife, Bebee, sat in an elevated office near the front door. The elevated office extended beyond the side walls out into the store, proper. In this way, Mr. Wallace and his wife could survey the work of their many employees.

146.

At its very heart, the Value Market was a family and James and Bebee Wallace were the caring parents. The store general manager,
Bob, was a lay minister at a local Free-Will Baptist church. When
Bob was not managing the employees, he was peering through
one-way mirrors in the store's back to catch shop lifters.

Bobby had arrived at seven o'clock one morning, a full hour before
the store opened. He sat in the Ford with the heater going reading
a rock-and-roll magazine. His studies at Northeast State were going well. He had never been a brilliant student, but he had a thing
for electonics. As Mr. Wallace unlocked the front door to Value Market, Bobby made his way to Veronica's cash register. He preferred
sacking groceries at her station over the other two cashiers. As he
placed the groceries in the paper sacks, he would take sneaking
peaks at the attractive red head. Veronica was divorced and age
thirty-five. She was a bit taller than Bobby and she had fair skin and
piercing but honest blue eyes. When Veronica looked at Bobby he
felt a thrill passing through him, lifting his spirits.

"Bobby, honey, could you take this bottle of Clorox bleach to aisle
five and exchange it for the generic bleach?" She asked , looking at
him.

The red head was well aware that the always attendant Bobby was
secretly in love with her.

"Right," he said and he felt a slight tremble as his hand barely
touched Veronica's fingers as he grasped the bottle.

Bobby had memorized every time he had touched those fingers.
The beauty of her hand had been branded into his mind forever.
As Bobby walked back to trade the Clorox for another bleach, he
reflected on things. As his hand had brushed up against Veronica's
small and tapered fingers, he had noticed that she had changed
her color of nail polish. He had felt for along time that she must be
seeing a manicurist. As a single working woman, Veronica allowed
herself few luxuries, but a professional nail person was something
she could afford. Usually, she wore bright red nails. Today, the
nails at the ends of her soft white hands were colored yellow,

accentuated with tiny blue stars.

The door to Bobby's room was closed. It was late at night on a weekend and his older brother had just returned from drinking. Seth did not make it up to his room in time. The screaming downstairs had begun between Seth and his father. Bobby put a pillow over his head, but to no avail. The raised voices and shouting were unrelenting and had been going on for months. The father and the elder son did not agree on many things. Bobby never crossed his father and rarely spoke to him. Frankly, Bobby knew that his father was volatile and unpredictable. He did not trust the old man. Seth was different and that was the problem. Bobby could hear his mother crying in the midst of all this. She and Seth were close. Eventually, quiet prevailed and Seth came upstairs. Bobby could sense the pain in his older brother's footsteps.

Bobby's older brother, Seth, was twenty-two and had been drinking since age seventeen. He had left two cars wrecked in steep ravines and had spent a few nights in jail. Seth had a fascination for knives, in fact, Seth had never hurt anyone.

Bobby knew that his father detested Seth, "but what else is new?" He told himself. The only person his father was good to was his wife. When Seth eventually moved out of the house, he went to public housing for the indigent. If Bobby thought Seth had it bad now, he knew that when he was young his father had it even worse.

"Was this an excuse for his father's behavior?" The nineteen year old wondered.

Autumn turned to Winter and Winter turned to Spring. The customer's from the projects began to walk to the Value Market rather than making the short drive. After all, city housing was right across the street from Value Market. The customers of the store were divided into three groups: single mothers, elderly women living alone and indigent families. Shorty's girlfriend was from one of the indigent families. She had just turned sixteen when Shorty met her in front of the meat counter. The blonde butcher was very talkative. When Sheila and her mother were choosing beef one morning, Shorty struck up a conversation with them. Although the butcher liked to talk to the mothers and their daughters, he was actually very shy. Sheila sensed the sincerity in Shorty's manner. Soon they were a couple.

Seth had come home in bad shape. The old man and his wife had already turned in for the night. The twenty-two year old was a roaring drunk as he stumbled through the darkness of the house. Stopping several times before climbing the stairs, he vomited all over the green carpet in the living room. Seth was not aware of his mental state and therefore was not motivated to clean up the mess. Bobby lay awake in his bed as he listened to the retching of his older brother. Once he knew Seth was in his own bedroom, Bobby went to check on him. Seth lay with his face to the ceiling, fully clothed on his bed. His flannel shirt was unbuttoned and open, exposing his chest to the stark evening light. The younger brother removed his Seth's boots, placing them under the bed. He then threw a blanket over the torso of his brother and retreated to his own room.

By virtue of the fact that he was completely soused, Seth slept soundly. The younger brother could hear the loud snore from his room down the hall. There was no window to Bobby's room, so it was dark when the solitary light was turned off. The nineteen year old liked it that way. He had spent his life pursuing obscurity and the shadows. Bobby did not like attracting attention. At nineteen, he had been in love with many women, most of whom he had never spoken to. He preferred divorced, older women, thirty to forty years of age, to become infatuated with. The teen-age girls and the girls in their twenties were too difficult to approach. These younger wom-en all chased the boys with rich daddies, who could hand over the keys to a new sports car to them.

Yes, Bobby was desperately in love with Veronica. He was also very preoccupied with a dark-headed, brown-skinned secretary at the community college-Melissa. One night he lay on his side reflecting on Melissa's silky, tanned legs. A woman's legs could be too plump or too thin. There was an in-between conformation that Melissa's legs typified. The curves of her calves and the taper of her thighs, below the short skirts that she wore had impressed him.   Whenever he was in class, his thoughts were on the shape of Melissa''s legs and her other fine features. His thoughts then wandered from the images of Melissa to what his life might be in the future.

He had one more year of community college. Then where would he move? There weren't many opportunities in Greenville. Greenville was rural, in the foothills of the Appalachian Mountains. The most mechanized industry in town was the meat-packing plant where undocumented, Mexican immigrants worked. Wherever he moved, perhaps to Charlotte or Richmond, he would know no one. "Couldn't be worse than living here," he grimly realized. Although his school tuition took most of his salary, he was methodically putting away the money that was left at the month's end.

At Value Market Bobby sacked groceries with gusto. From time to time, he would look up at Veronica at her cash register. When all the customers' bags were filled with groceries, and there was time, he would change places to arrange items on the "impulse shopper" counter near Veronica. Tonight she wore a sheer, off-white blouse with no sleeves. Her plump arms were very visible as he looked aside at her. Bobby tried to keep his eyes away from the front of her blouse where the top three buttons were temptingly unbuttoned. He stood there working, surveying the divorcee. Fearing that his interest in her would be given away, he eventually left the front and walked to the back of the store to talk to Shorty.

"Ten in aisle three," Shorty said as Bobby approached him.

"You aren't kiddin man," said the sack out boy. "I saw her with her mother and she is a ten if there ever was once," Bobby said.

150.

"Don't tell my girlfriend, Sheila, I said that, or you and I are history," Shorty warned.

"No problem, Shorty, we have an agreement on that one," Bobby assured the butcher.

"I heard last week that Mr. Wallace threatened to fire Bob," Shorty said in a low voice.

"Too many groceries walkin out the front door," Bobby said.

"Well, Bob ain't that bad at catching thieving. Yesterday he stopped an old woman with a fancy coat. When he made her open the coat, it was lined up and down with pockets filled with things the ol lady had filched," Shorty revealed.

"Say, Shorty...You and I are friends, aren't we?" Bobby asked.

"Absolutely, old man," Shorty replied.

"Take these thirty dollars and go to the flower shop for me," Bobby requested.

"Right, but why?" The butcher asked.

"Just go there and buy a bunch of yellow roses, with something to put them in, and put the whole thing at the end of Veronica's aisle on the day I give you the word, okay?" Bobby asked.

"Whatever," Shorty answered.

"Let me have a talk with you, young man," the request came from the corner of the room as Bobby headed toward the stairs to his bedroom.

Bobby looked into the dark of the room to see his father sitting in the corner. Bobby's mother had been in bed for hours. The time was

151.

midnight. His father had not aged well. Once fit and athletic, he
had now become increasingly out-of-shape. His wife had complained that he was eating himself to death. His weight had increased to the point that he had trouble getting up from a sitting
position. He walked with difficulty.

"Times are hard, son," his father complained. "You know that your
mother and I don't ask much of you, but...." Bobby's face hardened
as he expected to get a request for money..."We can't keep up the
house payments unless you and your brother do your share," the
older man explained.

This request from his father was the last thing the young man needed to hear. He was in school until the early afternoon, and then
he worked at Value Market until evening. Only after Value Market
closed, late at night, was he able to rest in his bedroom. Bobby
gritted his teeth and walked up the stairs without answering his
father.

That weekend, the electronics student stopped by a local night spot
to pick up a sandwich on his way home from Value Market. He sat
at the bar and ordered a pulled-pork barbecue sandwich. A juke
box played in the background. Bobby could not help but overhear
an argument that was progressing between two men sitting down
from him at the bar.

"I thought I just heard myself say, the Bears kin whip the Saints any
ol time they fell likit," he heard in a raised voice.

"Well, I got ten big ones that say you couldn't call a pig in a barn-
yard," was the quick reply.

"Yah, and like you are good for ten big ones," was the response.
"Yer the biggest loser in Greenville and ever one here knows that I
am right on that one," a large man shouted.

Bobby then looked over his shoulder to see Seth grab the collar of
a heavy-set man with a black, three-day stubble sitting next to him.

152.

"I am gonna have you for supper, fat man!" His brother cried, pulling the overweight man off his stool.

Bobby quickly saw that Seth would be the sure loser in the quarrel he had just picked. Seth's adversary had six inches and eighty pounds over the slight alcoholic. With a frightful cry, the larger man threw Seth onto the floor next to the bar. As Seth fell, he hit his head and became dazed. Quick to take the advantage, his opponent delivered three quick kicks of his right boot into the hapless face of Seth. The fight was over.

The owner of the bar and his stout bartender did not consider it worth their while to critique either man involved in the fight. After the winner paid his bill and left, the bartender picked Seth up and took him out to the front parking lot. He left Seth near a ditch fronting the road to the bar. Bobby acted like he did not know his brother and tried to ignore Seth's humiliating fate. He paid for his sandwich and then, he quietly left. Bobby knew that it was useless trying to rescue Seth. Seth's behavior had made it clear to him over the past five years that Seth could not be rescued by anyone. At three a.m. the next morning, lying awake in his room, Bobby heard the slow steps of his brother climbing the creaky wooden stairs to his bedroom.

Two mornings later, Veronica came to work fifteen minutes late. This was unusual for the sharp-tongued beauty since she was a stickler for efficiency. It was late March, and as she got out of her car, the air felt warmer than lately. The usual blustery wind was soft and mild that morning. Approaching the Value Market building she pushed the door open and walked to her cash register. She stood before her register and pushed the "on" button. The cash drawer sprang back toward her waist. Mr. Wallace gave her a green canvas bag with bills and change for the day. As Veronica took the bag from the store's owner and reached inside to retrieve the money, she saw a bouquet of yellow roses on a wire metal stand sitting nearby. On the top of the flowers was a white card with the words: "for my Veronica" scrawled across it. She felt confused.

153.

"No man has shown interest in me for years," she puzzled.

She glanced around the store to see who else had seen the roses. All the sack-out boys were with Bob getting their day's "talking to." As usual, the faithful Bobby approached the conveyor at her station and placed himself at its end, waiting for groceries. Veronica took the bouquet and placed it by her side, and without speaking, began the day's work.

The next several hours were long for the red-headed divorcee. Pushing prices rapidly into the keyboard of the register, she reviewed all the men she knew. Her keen eye surveyed the older male employees looking for signs regarding who might have a secret crush on her. None of them were acting suspicious.

"I pray to God it's not Bob," she moaned to herself.

Failing to find any clues by noon, she picked up the vase of yellow roses and took them over to Bobby.

"Bobby, baby...Could you get some water for these?" She asked.

The nineteen year old did not look up and smile as usual. He stared onto the conveyor and froze stiff.

"Honey, don't take things so serious. It won't take much time to take these to the back and get some water, please," she said.

Bobby slowly walked up to his idol and took the vase of roses in both hands, Then, he just stood there without moving or speaking.

"Really, honey, I guess I'll just have to do it myself!" Veronica snapped at him and she retrieved the precious flowers.

As the hours passed the cashier began to realize that the always friendly and cheerful Bobby had not said two words to her. He sacked furiously at his station and seemed ill at ease.

154.

"What is bothering him?" She wondered. "Could it be that horrible old father of his?" She asked herself. Finally, she was completely put out with him.

"Bobby, dear, march yourself over here to your Veronica, do you hear me? What is up with you, honey?" She pleaded.

As the guilty young man stood before her, his face turned a deep red color, and she could seen sweat pouring out of him. He mumbled some unintelligible sounds and froze in front of the thirty-five year old woman again. Suddenly, Veronica realized the truth behind Bobby's strange behavior. Pleasure flooded her mind and she smiled, while struggling to contain her delight. The lovely woman walked up to the boy and took his face in both hands, planting two kisses upon his flushed cheeks.

"You have always been my man, honey, and you will always be my man. Now go on home and come back tomorrow," she whispered to him.

Bobby never moved away from Greenville after this. Once he finished school and got his own place, he took any technical job he could get to say in the same town as the red-head at Value Market. He was wise enough to know that she was too old to be anything other than what she already was to him. He also knew that being near Veronica is where he would always be.

155.

156.

www.ingramcontent.com/pod-product-compliance
Lightning Source LLC
Chambersburg PA
CBHW031541310726
48971CB00008B/2576